The Chronicles of CC

War's Desolation

Frank Becker

Greenbush Press: Houston

Dear John & Carol
Thank you for fifty
years of friendship.
Frank

Greenbush Press
Spring, TX

Published simultaneously worldwide.

Becker, Frank
Series: "The Chronicles of CC"
Book One
War's Desolation / Frank Becker

ISBN 978-0-9836460-7-5
Library of Congress Control Number: 2013955494

Printed in the United States of America

War's Desolation
is for
Brother Al

Alexander W. Salay
Blessed Man Ministries
www.blessedman.org

"...and this desire on my part, exempt from all vanity of authorship, had for its only object and hope that it might be useful to others as a lesson of morality, patience, courage, perseverance, and Christian submission to the will of God."

—Johann Wyss, 1812
Author, "The Swiss Family Robinson"

The Star Spangled Banner
Francis Scott Key, 1814

Oh, say can you see by the dawn's early light
What so proudly we hailed at the twilight's last gleaming?
Whose broad stripes and bright stars thru the perilous fight,
O'er the ramparts we watched were so gallantly streaming?
And the rocket's red glare, the bombs bursting in air,
Gave proof through the night that our flag was still there.
Oh, say does that star-spangled banner yet wave
O'er the land of the free and the home of the brave?

On the shore, dimly seen through the mists of the deep,
Where the foe's haughty host in dread silence reposes,
What is that which the breeze, o'er the towering steep,
As it fitfully blows, half conceals, half discloses?
Now it catches the gleam of the morning's first beam,
In full glory reflected now shines in the stream:
'Tis the star-spangled banner! Oh long may it wave
O'er the land of the free and the home of the brave!

And where is that band who so vauntingly swore
That the havoc of war and the battle's confusion,
A home and a country should leave us no more!
Their blood has washed out their foul footsteps' pollution.
No refuge could save the hireling and slave
From the terror of flight, or the gloom of the grave:
And the star-spangled banner in triumph doth wave
O'er the land of the free and the home of the brave!

Oh! thus be it ever, when **freemen shall stand**
Between their loved home and the **war's desolation!**
Blest with victory and peace, may **the heav'n rescued land**
Praise the Power that hath made and preserved us a nation.
Then conquer we must, when **our cause it is just**,
And this be our motto: "In God is our trust."
And the star-spangled banner in triumph shall wave
O'er the land of the free and the home of the brave!

Broadcast Center

Chicago, Illinois
April 21st, 7:45 p.m.

It was late. The staff, including the daytime talent and the marketing people, had left for the day. Only the nighttime broadcast crew was on hand.

He too should have left hours before, but he had remained at his desk, glancing occasionally at his program notes, but really struggling to relate recent incidents in his life to the cataclysmic events occurring around the world.

Intuitively he felt that there had to be some relationship, but he didn't seem to have enough of the pieces to draw any meaningful conclusions. He leaned back in his chair, sighed deeply, and rubbed his eyes.

That day's program had been the most difficult he'd ever hosted. Things hadn't begun well. Although he was considered one of the most popular Christian talk show hosts in America, he had a relatively small staff, just a half dozen people, including a researcher, a call screener and a paid engineer.

The call screener was an unpaid volunteer, a double-amputee, and a veteran of the Afghanistan war. Although very faithful and reliable, he hadn't shown up that morning, nor had he called in with an explanation for his absence. As a result, the station had assigned a new employee to screen his calls. And from the moment he took his first call, it was obvious that the call screener was not sympathetic to his views. He couldn't shake the feeling that her assignment to his staff was intentional.

During the entire three-hour program, every call she routed to him was from someone antagonistic. He'd been at this a long time, and he had no difficulty at all picking out those callers that had an ax to grind, especially political operatives, atheists, and social activists who had been trained as spin doctors and in disinformations.

He wished that he could discuss what had been going on with his wife, but she was at home in Vermont, a long flight away. He decided to call her, but just as he was reaching for the phone, it began ringing. When he picked it up, the station manager's secretary told him that he was wanted. This in itself was unprecedented, because the station manager never worked after hours.

This was the talk hosts flagship station, the place where he produced his weekday broadcasts, and from which they were repeated around America and even in several other countries. The people who owned and managed it were his close friends and had always been devoted to the cause of Christ.

As he left his office, he was unaccountably troubled by the summons.

Definitely a problem, he thought. My ratings are up, I've been receiving emails and letters of praise from members of my listening audience, I've got more sponsors than I have spots available, and several more stations want to pick up the program. On the other hand, Congress has just passed a bill which is patently unconstitutional, but in effect gives the IRS and other agencies the power to close churches or replace their pastors if they are judged to be violating human rights. Has the president signed it? he wondered.

His thoughts raced. *Am I imagining things? If the anti-Christian crowd has gathered so much power that they can dictate what is preached in our churches, won't they also control Christian radio and TV? For years, they had condemned Christian "Millenialists" as dangerous, and denounced the Church for supposedly preaching hatred and terrorism. Was the attack on today's program an effort to embarrass Christian talk radio in general, and me in particular? And, if so, what's next?*

As he made his way down the hall, he was struck by the fact that two different studios had their *On Air* signs illuminated. Since only one studio could be on the air at any given moment, and the staff was forbidden to use the broadcast studios for production work, someone must be holding a private conversation in one of the sound-proofed rooms, and they had turned on the mic switch to light the hall sign. That would keep anyone who might be wandering the halls from bothering them, because it was forbidden to open a studio door when the *On Air* sign was illuminated.

He was mildly curious, but the venetian blind that covered the large studio window was tightly closed. As he passed the door, however, he got a glimpse through its narrow window, and recognized one of the two men who were in deep conversation.

The man looked up, and their eyes locked. The talk host started to smile in greeting, for he had interviewed this young politician just a few hours before, a man whose name was being bandied about as a possible presidential candidate.

The senator, however, appeared shocked, and tried to push away a thick packet of bills that was at that very moment being handed to him. The eyes of the man who was passing the senator the money followed his gaze toward the door, and he reacted by snapping something to an unseen person somewhere else in the room.

Do I know that guy? he wondered. *Sure. He's some Chinese bigwig.* Then he remembered. *He recently lost his diplomatic immunity, was ordered to leave the U.S., and is now persona non grata because he was caught spying. Yes, that's him! He was once glorified as a major industrialist, but it turned out that he had grown obscenely rich running unsafe industrial sweat shops, and he is also a general in the Chinese army.* His mind raced. *Since he's not supposed to be in the U.S.A., why would he be here at the station, and why would a senator be taking money from this avowed enemy of America?*

He didn't want to consider the obvious, but the newsman in him took control. He was reaching for the door handle when someone bumped into him from the rear, almost knocking him off his feet, and propelling him down the hallway. He turned, expecting to receive an apology, but all he got was a cold stare from a member of the station's security staff.

Something's definitely wrong!

He walked into the executive reception area, a forced smile on his face, and the secretary, usually very pleasant, simply pointed at the manager's door.

"He's waiting for you."

When he entered the office, he was surprised to find the network president sitting behind the general manager's desk. He had a phone to his ear, and his tone of voice indicated his unhappiness.

"Yes, I'll take care of it." He looked up to identify his visitor, then swiveled to his right and continued, "Yes, he's here now." Then, obviously annoyed with the caller's persistence, "I told you, I'll take care of it, McCord!" and slammed the phone down.

The broadcaster's eyes searched for those of the man behind the desk, but the executive seemed a different man, his gaze shifting about, unwilling to maintain eye contact with his visitor. A slight movement across the room caught the visitor's attention, and he turned to see the head of the station's small security force standing beside a well-dressed man, both of them staring across the room at him.

He turned back to the executive when, without so much as a greeting, the president stated flatly, "Your contract is terminated, effective immediately." Then, almost as an afterthought, "That includes the hundred odd stations that have been paying to carry your program."

The news was heart-stopping, and he hardly had time to take it in before the network president went remorselessly on.

"The secretary is preparing your final check. We're offering you an additional check as severance, but you have to understand that, since we won't be receiving any payment from your network affiliates, it won't amount to much." Then, as though it was of no significance, "And you will have to sign a document promising not to discuss with anyone anything concerning your work here, your relationship with the network, or the reasons for your termination."

He didn't know whether to sneer at the offer of severance, or to ask the reason for his abrupt termination. He instead found himself asking, "Why is the senator taking money from that ChiCom military industrialist?"

For the first time, his former friend appeared to really acknowledge him. Up until then, he had been speaking to him as dispassionately as a bank officer refusing a stranger a loan.

"I wish you hadn't asked that." There was a hint of sorrow in his voice. "Please gather your personal possessions and be out of the building within twenty minutes."

The executive nodded toward the uniformed officer, and

continued in what sounded like the poorly rehearsed dialogue for a bad movie. "This gentleman will remain with you while you gather your things. Also, it is requested that you avoid speaking with other employees or visitors."

"I don't understand, Tom. You and I have worked together for years. We have a track record of friendship and trust...."

The executive chopped his hand through the air like a cleaver, cutting him off.

"This is strictly business, and there is no point in painfully extending this conversation."

"That's not good enough, Tom. I deserve better than this."

"Well, if you are demanding an explanation, I refer you to the gentleman standing by the window, Mr. Sunfield of the I.R.S."

He turned toward the men standing across the room. "Ah," he rejoined, a wry smile on his face. "You're from the I.R.S., and you're here to help us, as the old joke goes."

"Actually," the agent said, moving across the room, "I'm here to arrest you, if you give us any trouble."

"On what grounds?"

"Trust me, we have legal ground." He pulled a document from his pocket, and extended it toward him.

"I'll take your word for it," he said, waving him off.

He returned his attention to the network president. "So that's it? That's all the explanation I'm going to get after eight years of faithful service?"

The executive pointedly stared at the face of his watch. "You have nineteen minutes remaining."

Without another word, he turned and left the room, the pneumatic door closing behind him, then hissing again as the big rent-a-cop followed in his wake, an appropriate sound under the circumstances.

He took the check the secretary held out to him, but when she handed him the disclaimer that the boss had mentioned, and ordered him peremptorily to "Sign on the bottom," he let it flutter to the floor, and turned away.

He was surprised to hear the cop say, "Maybe you don't need the money, but you'd be smart to cooperate."

He ignored him, and moved stiffly from the room.

He had walked the length of this same hallway a thousand times. The thickly carpeted corridors should have looked the same to him, but they did not. The costly wall coverings and muted lighting had taken on a joyless, if not sinister, cast, and the digitally produced broadcast emanating from the speakers in the ceiling reminded him that his own voice would no longer be heard anywhere in America. He was still in shock from the brief one-sided conversation. *What had gone wrong?*

As he approached the studio where he'd seen the senator and the general, he slowed.

As though anticipating his next move, the guard who was following him said, "Mind your own business. You don't work here anymore."

He slowed as he turned to speak to the man who towered over him.

There was a warning implicit in the other's question. "Haven't you ever heard that curiosity killed the cat? Literally?" Then the guard painfully grasped his upper arm in his massive hand, and almost dragged him past the studio door.

There were empty cardboard cartons stacked on his desk, and while he began searching the desk drawers and bookcases for items of a personal nature, his guard stood outside the door to keep inquisitive people away.

He picked up the phone, and pressed two buttons to speed dial his home number. The answering machine invited him to leave a message, but just as he started to do so, a hand reached around him and pressed the *Off* button. He turned in annoyance to see the guard standing next to him.

"No phone calls," he stated flatly.

His annoyance turned to incredulity, then anger, when he noticed the gun in the man's hand.

"What the...?"

"Just finish up, and get out of here."

The guard seemed to take no interest in the items he gathered, and it took him only a moment to finish. With a carton under one arm, and the handle of his laptop case in the other, he left the building.

The security guard stayed by his side until he'd gotten into his rental car and pulled out of the parking lot. Then he took out his cell phone, and punched in a number. A moment later, he said, "He's on his way," and hung up.

The subject of their conversation was driving back to his rental apartment to pack for his last flight home, when he turned a corner and saw a dump truck careening down the hill toward him. Without thinking, he yanked the wheel to the right. His car hit the curb hard, bounced violently, then skidded across the sidewalk to sideswipe an office building.

Thankfully, the airbags weren't activated. Momentarily dazed, he finally got out of the car and turned to look for the dump truck. It was about a fifty yards down the hill, on the far side of the intersection, its front axle jammed over the top of a broken water main.

The truck driver jumped down from the cab into several inches of swirling water, and began yelling at him that he should wait for him so that they could exchange insurance information.

He waved his hand to signify agreement. As he started down the hill to join the driver, he saw the man's feet swept out from under him, and as he reached out to cushion his fall, he dropped something into the water.

The driver of the auto pivoted, and started back toward his car. *I'm not a kid anymore, but my vision hasn't become so poor that I can't tell the difference between an insurance ID card and a handgun.* He reached into his car, grabbed his laptop, and started running up the hill away from the truck.

The Script Kiddie

Saugerties, NY
April 22nd, 9:00 a.m.

It was Saturday morning and the teenager had spent nearly an hour wandering aimlessly around the village, seemingly studying the historic buildings.

Saugerties lies on the west bank of the Hudson River, a little north of the half-way point between New York City and Albany. Settled in the early 18th century, it had become a small thriving industrial and shipping center, but by the 1970s, most of its industry and population had drifted away on the tides of change. Economic conditions again reversed about the time of Jonathan's birth, when Saugerties, like nearby Woodstock, became popular with commuters from New York City. They were drawn to its rural setting and low-cost real estate, and it began to flourish as an art colony and tourist center.

Of singular interest to Jonathan, however, was the presence of an eccentric young software engineer who had rejected what he called the forty-hour-a-week enslavement to the world of information technology in order to operate what appeared to be a failing business in a run-down storefront. Not suffering fools gladly, he had a reputation for throwing customers out of his shop. Most people in town thought he would soon be out of business, unaware that he'd produced numerous products that resulted in a very hefty income stream.

Jonathan, wearing a windbreaker and baseball hat, and sporting dark sunglasses, sauntered along Main Street, pretending to examine items in various store windows. He was actually checking the reflections of people around him, occasionally looking over his shoulder to determine whether someone might be following him. His attempt to disguise himself was not without justification. His best friend had just been arrested for attempting to hack into government websites, and he had good cause to be concerned about being implicated.

When he reached the middle of the 200 block, he turned to examine the buildings on the far side of the street. His eyes settled momentarily on a dilapidated store-front. Its cracked plate glass window was blanked on the inside by a grid of white poster board sheets taped to the grimy glass. Someone had used a felt marker to scribble "CyberSpace Corp" in one corner, a pretentious name for what appeared to be a failing startup.

Jonathan abruptly crossed the street, jogged between two moving cars, and leapt safely onto the opposite sidewalk. He took one more look up and down the street, then pushed open the door of the messy little shop. The store was small, with just a few feet separating the front door from a service counter. Behind the counter, shelves were stacked floor-to-ceiling with obsolete computers and monitors, framing a steel door that led to a back room. He hadn't spoken, but suddenly a disembodied voice asked, "What's up, Jonathan?"

"I wondered if I could ask you a few questions."

"I dunno, kid. Having you in my shop is likely to get me in trouble."

"What do you mean?" he replied, though he was sure he knew exactly what the speaker meant. Then, with a catch in his voice, "How did you find out?"

"Trust me, kid. I know what's going on."

Suddenly he heard the sound of a magnetic catch being released, and the voice ordered, "Come on in, kid."

He stepped through the door, and it clicked shut behind him. The back room was in radical contrast to the rundown front room of the store, with its cracked plaster, peeling paint, and ancient light fixtures. This room was beautifully decorated, complete with plush carpeting and cool, filtered air. But what really set it apart were the furnishings. Jonathan had never imagined a more glamorous desk assembly, all solid hickory. Next to his keyboard, a name plate read "Jamie Edwards."

The man he'd come to see was sitting in a leather recliner. He had a computer keyboard, track ball, and remote-control device resting on a counter elevated just above his lap, like the shelves that rotated above hospital beds. Before him, suspended from the back wall, were two rows of large flat-panel monitors, a total of six, fixed in a rectangular grid.

As Jonathan scanned the screens, he could see that one

was open to email, another to news feeds, and still others to strange programming applications. As he was trying to make sense of them, his host pressed a button on his keyboard, and the screens went dark. Then he pivoted his work counter out of the way, and rose from the chair.

The teen turned to follow the man's movements. He was reaching into a small refrigerator that was built into the solid hickory cabinets that covered the entire wall.

"Wow," the boy exclaimed. "Everyone in town thinks you're near bankruptcy." He shook his head. "This must have cost a fortune."

"Yes. I had to bring in someone from out of town to build it in order to keep those rumors going."

He handed Jonathan a soft drink. His hospitality was gracious. His words were not.

"Okay, straight answers only," the man said. "Did you at any time join your friend while he was trying to hack any websites?"

"How did you know about that?"

"You'd be surprised what I know. Now, answer the question."

As Jonathan responded, he ceased eye contact and looked off to the left.

Is the kid going to lie to me? he wondered. *Is he afraid or ashamed, or is he simply looking inward and thinking over his response.* The boy's reply seemed evasive, and he was not encouraged.

"Well," he responded, "he didn't try to hack any government websites."

"That's not what I asked. Were you ever there while he was trying to hack anybody's site?"

"Yes, the school website."

The man shook his head, a look of disgust, or perhaps disappointment on his face.

"D-U-M-B," he spelled out. "Did you personally access or make use of any information that your pal accessed?"

"No!" he answered, his voice suddenly defiant. "I told him to back out and leave it alone, and he did."

"Okay. Just maybe you're okay."

He stared into Jonathan's eyes. "You are absolutely certain you were never there while he was trying anything else?"

He didn't hesitate this time. "Yes, I'm certain. He wanted me to work with him to try to hack government sites, but I was too scared."

"A good thing, too. He's definitely going to jail."

Jonathan gulped. "But he's only sixteen."

"The law is the law, kid, and ignorance of the law is no excuse. The question is whether you will be considered an accessory before, during, or after the fact."

"I didn't realize it was that bad."

"I hate to say it kid, but I don't want you coming around here any more."

"But I need your help. This is important."

"Not to me, it's not. I've got a good life, and I'm one of the good guys. I don't need some script kiddie dragging me under."

"But you told me...."

"Forget what you think I told you!"

"I'm sorry."

"You'd better be sorry. If you're not now, you will be."

"But I need to know...."

"What do you need to know?"

"I think that America's in trouble. I wanted to try to hack some websites to find out."

"What websites? Why would you want to do that?"

"To find out whether we might be attacked, in order to get ready."

"Well, if we are attacked, and I'm not saying we won't be, you don't want to be in jail when it happens."

"So what do I do? I've read everything you've given me on hacking."

"Listen to me, Jonathan. You can't learn to be a hacker by reading books. You have to actually work at it to learn how. It's like being a football coach, or a brain surgeon, or painting landscapes. Yes, it's a science, but it's an art too. It takes intuition and smarts and above all, constant effort."

"But you gave me a reading list. You told me to study the stuff."

"To learn the theory, sure! But that's it. If you try to go further than that, you're going to wind up in jail."

The boy was downcast.

"Look kid, becoming a hacker is a long-term job. And if you're right about a war, it will start years before you can learn how." *It's apt to start in the next few hours,* he almost added.

"I don't understand."

The man didn't attempt to hide his impatience.

"This isn't a game, Jonathan. True hackers are generally professionals with years of training, and most are not criminals, although in some countries, like communist China, Russia, and Saudi Arabia, the governments actually sanction and pay for attacks on the networks of other nations."

"I've read that."

"Well, it's true. Nations can rise or fall as a result of electronic espionage. And you are a fool if you become involved."

"Aren't you a hacker?"

"Sure. But what you don't seem to understand is that all 'hackers' aren't engaged in illegal activities."

"No?"

"No! Not all hackers are bad. Many explore and build code themselves. The White-Hat hackers are often hired to promote security by penetration testing. Pen testing is attacking a system as if you were a bad guy, but you're not. You're just looking for flaws so that it can be improved. That's what I generally do."

"Like beta testing?"

"No. Beta testing is used in the development of an application. When someone employs pen testing, it's generally on an existing and operating website."

"Oh."

"Black-Hat hackers are the ones who penetrate sites illegally. The media lumps all hackers together and uses the black-hatters to defame all the others. That's why most people think of all hackers as bad guys. "

"That's it?"

"No, then there are the Grey-Hat hackers. Those are something in-between...."

"But the laws!" the boy expostulated.

"Right. Once upon a time, hackers used their skills to break into computer networks. They'd leave an anonymous email for the system administrators—the sysadmins—to let them know they'd been 'p0wned', and they even provided directions on how to fix the problems they'd uncovered. It was a game, a huge game, and it was generally very beneficial to government and industry. But now the government had foolishly made all hacking criminal and even labeled it as terrorism, regardless of the hacker's intent, and they've legislated away one of the key tenets of *mens rea.*

"What's mensre, or whatever you called it?"

"*Mens rea.* When a court deals with a crime, they are generally concerned with motive. Motive, opportunity, and weapon. The Black Hat uses a computer as a weapon, and his skill, coupled with access to the Internet, provides the opportunity. His determination to steal information or bring down a website would be considered his motive. Today the act alone is sufficient to send him to jail."

"I don't get it."

"Mens rea is an element of criminal responsibility. It has to do with a guilty mind; a guilty or wrongful purpose; a criminal intent. Under the new laws, however, it doesn't matter what your motives are. If you hack, you've committed a crime. Period!"

"So hackers don't dare penetrate networks anymore?"

"Well, the White Hatters can hack the network of the company they work for or contract to, under supervision, with written authorization, with the intent of testing the system. The thing is that true hackers are justifiably proud of their work," he continued, "and are sensitive about how the word hacker is used."

"Well, what can I do then?" the boy asked.

"It's really simple. If you want to know what's about to happen in the world, start lurking on Fritter, URC, and similar websites so that you can start to feel the winds of change—'chatter' in the parlance of DHS. Oh, and check the Grudge Report."

"That's it?"

"That's all I'm giving you, Jonathan. And it's good advice. Do you understand?"

"Yeah, I guess so." He bit his lip, kicking his toe against the carpet. "So now what?"

The man opened a closet in the back of the room, and removed a small carton.

"Take this with you."

The boy glanced at the box. "A wireless router?"

"Yes. If anyone asks what you were doing here, just tell them you were buying this. That might just save us both from criminal action."

"What do I owe you?"

"Nothing, Jonathan. Just get out of here and don't come back."

"Never?"

"Jonathan, I'll give you this much." He frowned, hesitating to go further. Then he muttered something like, "Oh, what the hay." He put his hand on the boy's shoulder, and stared into his eyes. "You're right, Jonathan. War is imminent. So you won't be coming back here again. We might not even survive it. But I don't want you to be arrested before you have the opportunity to try."

He opened the door to the front room.

"Go home, keep an eye on the right websites, get ready for what's coming, maybe scrape out a corner in one of your father's mushroom caves, and trust God."

As Jonathan stepped out onto the sidewalk, he suffered conflicting feelings. His strange friend had just confirmed his worst suspicions, but he'd also freed him from the need to expose himself to arrest. He turned away and started up the street.

Then it occurred to him. *He knew that my father grows mushrooms.* When he turned back to reenter the store, an old-fashioned pull-down shade had been drawn down behind the glass in the door, and when he tried to turn the handle, he found that it was locked. Then he noticed the words printed neatly on the shade. "Closed. Gone Out of Business."

Hidden Valley

Central Vermont
April 22nd, 6 p.m.

While one man was surveying the death of his career, and those who had been orchestrating his ruin were seeking shelter in diverse places, a far-seeing farmer and his wife were also preparing for the possibility of holocaust.

"Try to hurry, Sandra!"

"Oh, Joseph, is this really necessary?"

"If not for us, then for Sarah."

He started walking across the pasture. "I'll go get the horses and the cow. You gather the sheep and goats." They could hear Sarah already driving the poultry before her, and smiled at her enthusiasm.

"All right, Joseph."

"We have to hurry before it's too dark to see these critters," he laughed. Then he added, "As soon as we get the two of you settled, I'll head for the co-op."

"But they'll be closed for the weekend," she protested.

"And if matters are as urgent as you make them sound, is it prudent for you to go today?"

"If I don't," he responded, we won't have adequate feed for the animals. And don't worry, Don will open the store for me."

The Opportunist

Baltimore, MD
April 22nd, 6:30 p.m.

McCord spoke a name into his smart phone, and when the correct contact information appeared, he pressed the call button. After it rang four times, and he was shunted to voice mail, McCord left his name and number and hung up.

He owes me, he thought, but that doesn't mean he'll be prone to pay me back.

Three minutes later, the colonel returned his call.

"Jimmy, how are you?" he asked in that remarkably charming voice he invariably used to disarm others.

"Hey, Unk, I'm hoping you're going to help me get out of Dodge," McCord responded without any preliminaries.

"Get out of Dodge? I'm not sure I know what you're talking about."

"Sure you do. We both know that some nasty things are about to happen, and before they do, I want you to take me along to wherever it is you're going. Some place safe and cozy."

"What makes you think I'm going anywhere," his uncle asked, his voice now cold and dangerous. "Or," he continued, "that I'd take you along if I were going anywhere? You may be my sister's son, but you've done very little to endear yourself to me."

"Okay, forget the blood-is-thicker-than-water thing. You and I go back a long way. And I pulled your chestnuts out of the fire more than once."

"The question. my dear nephew, is, 'What have you done for me today?'

"What do you mean? I did what you asked. I had the guy in Vermont taken care of."

"I told you to take care of the matter personally."

"You know that I don't do that kind of work."

"You mean you're afraid to get your hands dirty."

"I mean that my skills lie in other areas."

"Or maybe you're just afraid."

"So what's the problem. I hired the best man available."

"Well, for your information, he failed."

"What?"

"The best man available didn't finish the job."

"His family is dead, right? And he's ruined...."

"But he's still alive."

"So what? By tomorrow he'll be toast too."

"Maybe, but he seems to have nine lives, and I didn't want to have to count on tomorrow."

McCord's thinking took a new twist. "This isn't really about any threat this guy might represent to your plans, is it?"

Now the colonel's voice took on a hint of menace as he ground out his reply in a whisper.

"What are you trying to say?"

"I've got ears. I've picked up the gossip?"

"Indeed. And you do know how I react to people gossiping about me, don't you Jimmy?"

McCord was now so full of himself that he did not see the trap yawning wide before him. His uncle's words, and his even gentler tone, should have been a warning to McCord, but instead he saw them as a form of capitulation. He exulted that he might have exerted some small control over the colonel, so he pushed blindly ahead.

"Yes. And I know you have a personal vendetta against him that goes back to your college years."

The colonel remained silent.

"Well?"

"Well, what, Jim?"

"How about helping me get out of town?"

"It's true that you've done me a favor once or twice, but...."

"Absolutely! So tell me where I should meet you."

"Now you wait a minute...."

"No, you wait. There are some people that are still trying to understand where you fit in on the Eng espionage business, and I'm just the guy to tell them."

"No need to make threats, Jim. And, as you suggested, it probably won't matter after tomorrow anyway. And, to your point, blood is really thicker than water, so for old times sake, I'm sure we can work something out."

"I'm waiting."

"Okay. Actually your call is very timely."

"How so?"

"Well, I'm just about get out of DC myself."

"And?"

"Can you meet me and my family at SuperJet Aviation at BWI by noon?"

"You're leasing a plane?"

"No, I have a contract with SuperJet to service my plane at their facilities."

"Oh, nice. Your own jet."

"Yes," he replied smugly. "Life's been good to me."

"I'm sure it has," McCord agreed, the irony unmistakable. "I'll meet you at SuperJet before noon."

"Don't be late, Jimmy. I'd hate to have to leave without you."

Before he could respond, the colonel had hung up. As McCord pressed the *End Call* button on his cell phone, he wondered whether he would survive any assistance that the colonel might offer.

The Siblings

Deep River Junction
April 22nd, 8:12 p.m.

When her father had called to insist she bring the two children for a visit, it didn't seem a problem to Chris. Her husband was to be away until late Friday night or Saturday, and since she home-schooled her two young children, it would be no problem taking them away for a few days. In fact, it would be a great opportunity for them to gain more firsthand knowledge of life on a homestead.

Regrettably, what had started as a pleasant day proved far more challenging than she'd imagined. She had taken the children to the store to pick up a few things for their trip upstate, and when they'd returned home, she found the light flashing on the answering machine, but no message. It couldn't have been her husband calling, she thought, for he'd have tried her mobile phone as well. But when she did get around to checking it, she discovered that the battery was dead.

The children were disappointed because they probably missed talking to their daddy. She assured them that she'd plug her phone into the car charger as soon as they left for grandpa's and grandma's, but in the confusion of loading up their suitcases, toys, and the cooler chest, not to speak of two excited children, she again forgot about it.

She was about ten miles north of town before she realized that she'd left a few very important items at home. Her husband had impressed upon her the need to be prepared for any emergency, and not merely earthquakes, hurricanes, and tornadoes. They'd been watching the news carefully as the international political and economic picture had become increasingly confused, and they'd both became very concerned when a few world leaders began rattling missiles. As a result, he had repeatedly warned her never to get more than a couple of miles from home unless she took both the package that was locked in the safe plus the emergency backpacks. And though she hated to waste almost an hour of back-and-forth driving, she knew that he was right. So, in spite of the children's grumbling, she turned the car around and headed back home.

The emergency packs were something her husband had put together a couple of years earlier and periodically updated. Each one consisted of a backpack and a sleeping bag. Each pack contained packages of light-weight freeze-dried food, a couple of bottles of water, first-aid supplies, a walkie talkie, a small radio, camping supplies, clothing, paper money, a few silver coins, and anything unique to each person's needs, such as medications. In addition, her backpack contained both pepper spray and a handgun with fifty rounds of ammunition.

It was the package in the safe, however, that her husband had impressed upon her as perhaps being most important. It contained cash, a roll of real silver quarters, plus photocopies of passports, birth certificates, their marriage license, insurance documents, credit cards, and bank account information, plus a DVD containing hundreds of family photos, and video clips of their home and possessions. Some of these items might prove both irreplaceable and vital, but he put the greatest emphasis on the silver coins.

"As far as the world is concerned, money talks," he'd told her. "And history shows that in the event of hyperinflation, one real silver coin might become worth more than a wheelbarrow heaped with worthless paper dollars." As she turned the car back toward home, she decided to add their laptop computer to the list. It too contained valuable family information that she wouldn't want to fall into the hands of identity thieves.

It was almost nine when she finally arrived back at the house, so she left the car in the driveway with the children asleep on the back seat. She was surprised to discover that the porch light was out, but she found her way to the door by the dim glow of the street light on the corner. *I just replaced that bulb the other day,* she thought, as she grasped the door handle, and poked around to get her key in the lock. She was startled when she heard a slight rustling in the shrubbery, and reached into her handbag for her container of pepper spray. Hearing nothing more, she assumed it had been a stray animal. As she started to turn the key, the doorknob turned with it, and she realized that the door was already open. *That's odd,* she mused, *I'm sure I locked it.*

The living room was dark, the only illumination a warm glow from a lamp that spilled through from their bedroom door. *I didn't leave the bedroom light on,* she thought. She slipped quietly to the center of the living room, but hesitated to call out. From there, she moved down the hall, pepper spray in hand. She could see through the open bedroom door where a dim aura surrounded their bed. She sensed rather than saw movement. There was a gleam of flesh, the sheen of satin, and a hint of musk. She could actually see very little, but her imagination filled out the picture. Then something alien, a disjointed movement in the unaccustomed gloom, a soft husky laugh, so familiar, yet so wrong here. The idea of someone in her bed filled her with intense revulsion and anger, and her anger turned to rage when she recognized her sister's laugh.

Michelle, she thought bitterly. She loved her sister, and they had shared many adventures through life, but she sometimes despised her for her immorality, while her sister in her turn mocked her as a goody-goody.

As she scrambled for the light switch, she shouted, “What are you doing in my bedroom?”

“Chris? It's just me, Michelle.”

“I know who it is. Who's that with you?”

There was the sound of someone snatching up clothes, then the bathroom door closing.

“It's...a...no one you know. A friend.”

“A friend? Why are you with 'a friend' in my bed, and why aren't you with your husband in your own apartment? And, who's taking care of your kids?”

"We couldn't meet at my apartment," Michelle responded.

"Why not?"

The answer didn't come for a moment. "Well, because he and his wife live right across the hall, and she would find out."

"So you're an adulteress now...."

"Keep your voice down; the kids will hear."

"Why should I keep my voice down? It's my house."

"I just don't want you to wake the kids."

"You mean that you brought your two kids over here? Your kids are asleep in my children's beds, while you...."

"Well, sure," she answered. "Why not," as though the answer should be obvious to anyone. "A good mother wouldn't leave her children home alone."

"A good mother?" Chris was grinding out the words, trying and failing to keep her anger under control. "A good mother wouldn't take her children with her while she shacks up with a married man at her sister's house."

"Okay, so a good mother wouldn't, but I don't have a husband like you do."

"You might have had, if you hadn't slept around on him."

"I didn't do anything he wasn't already doing."

Chris took a deep breath, trying to get her temper under control. *It's All right to be angry,* she thought, *but we're not to become sinful.* She counted to three, took a deep breath, and spoke in the calmest voice she could muster. "I want you, and whoever is cowering in my bathroom, to get out of my house! Do you hear me?" She was shouting again. "Right now!"

"Oh, come on Chris," Michelle appealed.

Chris had noted the slur in her sister's voice, and realized she'd been drinking again.

"Can't my kids just sleep with yours tonight? I don't want to wake them up."

"I repeat, I want you all out of here right now." She realized she was shouting now.

A voice came from down the hall. "Mommy, what is it? You're scaring me."

"Go back to sleep, honey." Then to Chris, "Now you see what you've done?"

"What I've done? You get that man out of my house before our neighbors see him. And you get those kids up, and get out of here."

As she finished making these demands, an unshaven middle-aged man with thinning disheveled hair, and shirt unbuttoned, appeared in the bathroom door with his shoes in hand. "I'm sorry," he mumbled. "I'm just on the way out." He walked quickly through the house, and let himself out the front door.

Her sister called after him, "I'm sorry, Ben. Will I see you later?"

"I'll try and come back after your prissy sister leaves."

"Don't you dare," Chris shouted after him.

As the screen door slammed, she heard him holler something profane. She hoped that her own kids were still asleep in her car, and were spared this scene.

Michelle, however, remained combative. "Now see what you've done?"

"Yes, and none too soon, obviously."

"All right, I'll leave. Just let me get dressed and I'll get the kids up. Can we talk first?"

"No. I'm not in the mood to talk to you. I'm going to grab a few things and head for dad's farm." It suddenly occurred to

Chris that a trip to the farm might be just the thing her sister needed.

"Do you want to come along?"

"In the shape I'm in? I'm not about to sit around for a couple of days while mom and dad lecture me."

"Maybe that's just what you need."

"You have no idea what I need!"

"Oh, of course not." She looked searchingly at her sister. "I was going to say that you're too drunk to drive, but it's obvious that if Mister Wonderful comes back tonight, you'll let him in."

"You can lay money on it."

"In that case, and in spite of my concern for your kids, I want you to leave right now."

"Oh, thanks!" The sarcasm dripped. "You mean that I get to go home and sleep alone."

"Exactly."

Without another word, Michelle began picking up her clothes from where they lay here and there around the room, and began dressing. She called down the hall, "Get dressed kids. We're going home."

"Oh, mom, do we have to?"

"Yes, we have to."

Without another word, Michelle left the room and went down the hall to gather her two children.

"Are you sure you don't want to come along to grandpa's farm?" Chris called down the hall.

"Absolutely! I don't need mom and dad tell me how to live. I've had it!" Then she took the kids by the hands and stormed out of the house.

Chris waited until she heard the sound of the car moving

away from the house, then stepped into her walk-in closet. *I'll grab a few things, and I'll be out of here,* too, she thought.

She left the bedroom with the package from the safe, and then headed for her country kitchen where the emergency packs hung on hooks near the back door. She loaded everything into the back of her SUV, and headed for 91 north.

About two minutes after Chris drove away, several people exited a darkened car that was parked about a block down the street, and moved through the shadows toward her house.

Arson Investigation

Deep River Junction, Vermont
April 22nd, 10:10 p.m.

Men in shiny yellow slickers moved cautiously among the soaking embers. Smoky vapor drifted wraith-like in the glaring lights.

One of the firemen, searching among the ruins, heaved a plank up and over, dumping a heap of charred and soggy refuse. Three ambulances were backed diagonally to the curb, their rear doors flung wide, awaiting the deposit of the human ruins that had been discovered among the ashes.

As the fire was quenched, so was the enthusiasm of the crowd that had gathered earlier to watch the house burn. They'd finally gone home, discouraged by the dampness, the stench, the evening chill, the presence of death, and the late hour.

As the EMS people went about their grisly task, a man drew his car to the curb and sat staring through his open window at the nightmarish scene. His hands twisted about the wheel, knuckles knotted and white in the unnatural light, face lost in the shadows.

Toward the back of the house, a fireman, having attracted a police officer's attention, pointed through the ruins toward a massive basement room. It had not completely resisted the enormous heat generated by the fire because its massive vault-like door had been left ajar. It was so quiet that the man in the car could hear the surprised exclamations of the fireman.

“Would you look at this, sheriff? Check out the cases of food stacked in there?”

The cop was unimpressed. “Yes. It's a safe room.”

“Safe room?”

“Yeah. You know. A safe room, sort of like a fallout shelter.”

The firemen shook his head, admitting his ignorance.

“It's a place to go during hurricanes, tornadoes, and even wars. It serves as an emergency shelter.”

“Oh, yeah” the fireman responded doubtfully. “I've heard of them, but I've never seen one.”

The sheriff laughed. “The people who build them generally don't advertise the fact.”

“Why not?”

“Because they wouldn't want ten thousand people trying to break into a shelter they designed and equipped when those unprepared souls suddenly found themselves caught in an emergency.”

The fireman pondered that for a moment.

“Yeah, sure. That makes sense.” He was staring at a gun rack that hung just outside the entrance to the shelter and held the remains of a couple of ruined shotguns. The wooden stocks were partially burned away, and the barrels and actions were hanging askew, already brown with rust. "Nobody's going to use those guns anytime soon," he observed. He looked at the cop. "Why would anyone want to own a gun?"

The sheriff groaned at the abysmal ignorance of his fellow public servant. "Lots of people own firearms. Some of us like to hunt. Others want guns for competitive target shooting. And some believe they need them for self defense."

"Self defense? From who?"

"Oh, thieves, rapists, those types. And some have the idea that if there were to be some sort of national crisis, they'd want to be able to defend themselves or help in the defense of our country."*Maybe a national emergency produced by some megalomaniac who wants to overthrow the government,* he thought, but he didn't share the thought with this guy. The sheriff studied the fireman as he continued to peer at the safe room, his mouth hanging open. *This fellow isn't the shiniest dime on the block,* the cop concluded, *but he's well-fitted for his job.*

"Do you go along with that, sheriff? The self-defense thing, I mean?"

"Sure, why not?"

"You're supposed to keep the peace. Doesn't it scare you that people might have guns?"

"Well, right off the bat, the U.S. Constitution, with good reason, guarantees the right of the individual citizen to keep and bear arms. Apart from that, the old saying is really true."

"What's that?"

"When guns are outlawed, only outlaws will have guns."

"Oh, I think that's dumb," the younger man responded.

"Well, think of the mass killings that have taken place

around the United States, in shopping centers, schools, theaters, even on military reservations," the sheriff reminded him. "If there'd been one civilian in any of those situations who was carrying a loaded weapon, they might have brought down the shooters before they killed so many people."

"Or," the fireman said, "they might have shot some of those innocent people."

"That's unlikely," countered the sheriff. "And proper training helps. One thing's sure, however."

"What's that?"

"Even if the civilians weren't great shots, unlike the bad guys, they wouldn't have been intentionally aiming at innocent people."

"Yeah, I guess that's true," the fireman grudgingly conceded.

"As it is," the sheriff continued, on the edge of letting his annoyance with this man's ignorance become evident, "many people have been killed because there was no one there to stand up for them. If you were caught in one of those situations, wouldn't you want someone with a weapon who might save your life?"

"Yeah, I suppose I would," the fireman agreed.

The sheriff searched his face and realized that, like most Americans, he had no idea how important these constitutional safeguards were to the preservation of a free state.

"The founding fathers included the right to keep and bear arms because they had just forcefully separated the United States from the rule of an oppressive government, a government that tried to take their guns away."

"I didn't know that, about the guns I mean." He thought

for a moment. "How could a few men with guns stand against a disciplined army?"

The sheriff laughed. "How could a few men stand against a disciplined army? The answer lies in the fact that they did." Then he summed it up. "A man defending his home and family will sacrifice a great deal more than a man who marches under orders for pay."

"I guess...."

"And that brings us back to your question about guns."

"What about them?"

"When things go wrong, when there's a disaster like a hurricane, earthquake, tornado, chemical spill, or a war, people can't really expect firemen and cops—you or me—to be available to come to their doors to help them. We will, very likely, be occupied elsewhere."

"That's true," the fireman answered. "I never thought of that. We could be tied up for days." The young fireman's eyes returned to the shelter. "Jeez Louise," he exclaimed, "those walls must be nearly two feet thick!"

"Yes," the sheriff conceded. "The people who built that shelter knew what they were doing. Those walls would stop a lot of radiation." He gnawed his lip. "The owner of this house cared about his family, and obviously spent a lot of time and money preparing for the worst."

"I think he was nuts."

"Why?"

"We'll never have an emergency that would justify that expense. And look what happened to them! Dead in an accidental fire."

"Are you sure it was accidental?"

"Well, that's a good question. I've got to admit, it sure

looks fishy. I guess we'll have to wait for the fire marshal's report."

The sheriff nodded his head, and continued his walk around the perimeter of the house. He was looking for the point at which the fire started, but he stopped for a moment to reflect on the investment these people had made to secure their lives, and how it all had evidently come to nothing.

Yet, judging from the way the man had provided fire extinguishers and smoke detectors, it was difficult to understand why no one got out alive. He already suspected that the fire was not accidental.

Private Jet

Chicago to New York City
April 22nd, 10:17 p.m.

The aged general had experienced the horror of the dream countless times over the past forty years. *Will I ever,* he often wondered, *be free of the terror of my step-father's curse?*

Once again he was caught up in the recurring nightmare. He was in his step-father's steel foundry, held immobile by his bodyguards, on a platform high above a crucible of molten steel. The flaring heat of the liquid metal below made the undulating shadows that surrounded him all the more impenetrable.

He was being forced to watch as his friend and co-conspirator—face and naked torso dripping with sweat and blood—babbled out his confession of betrayal. The moment that the truth was torn from his friend's mouth, his father nodded, and the screaming man was cast from the platform to the sea of molten metal below, his body exploding in flaming death, turning to a flaming cinder even as it seemed to be absorbed by the incandescent pool. His step-father seemed to savor the scene as he leaned over the railing, watching until the glowing surface was once again smooth and undisturbed.

Then he turned his all too familiar and merciless glare on him. But was there something more? Eng dared not hope that, perversely, there was just a hint of respect in his riveting stare. No, for with a flick of his eyes, his step-father sealed his fate, and his bodyguards lifted him above the railing. As he hung there, suspended between heaven and hell, he continued to stare into his step-father's eyes, refusing to struggle or scream, while the men who painfully gripped his wrists and ankles, awaited their lao ban's final order.

The man's eyes searched those of the son of his concubine, gazing in fascination as the expression on his rebellious step-son's face metamorphosed, his rebellion and hatred overcoming his fear. Instead of confessing his deceit, his son had persisted in denial. He had surrendered his honor, and would forever after live a lie. *He is mine now!* his step-father exulted. And rather than casting him after his co-conspirator into what he'd laughingly referred to as "The Dragon's Mouth," where the dross of guilt and sin would have been burned away, he was satisfied that the young man was forever recast in the mold of betrayer.

He waved his hand, and his bodyguards easily lifted the young man back over the railing to stand once again on the platform. Reaching for the railing to still his shaking hands, and with the bodyguards holding him gingerly, his step-father again questioned him.

"You, the illegitimate son of my concubine, dared murder my true son?" The question was clearly rhetorical. The older man lifted his head and spread his arms as though to embrace not just the steel mill, but all his considerable industrial enterprises that seemed to blanket China. "Did you honestly believe that you might inherit all this?"

The young man dared not speak, his eyes on the floor, as his step-father continued. He was shocked by his next words.

"It is just as well. I married because my wife's family would bring me vast industrial holdings, but her son was a weakling. You have conveniently rid me of him. You are the son of the woman I would have chosen, and you have revealed both your strength and your ruthlessness. You've proven yourself to be a man of some small courage and decisiveness. You are the kind of man I must have to manage these enterprises once I am gone, and the kind of man the new China will need to rule the world."

He pulled himself erect, and pointed into his step-son's face. "But don't think that you will do away with me the way you did your half-brother. When I am ready, and only then, you will be handed the reins of my empire."

With an exultation impossible to describe—having just moved from imminent death to what he considered a glorious new life—the young man bowed to feign his acquiescence.

Now, decades later, as he rocked back and forth in his sleep, he cried out at his own perfidy. His step-father had been wrong. He had been able to seize the reins of power long before he was prepared to yield them. Ironically, without his step-father's assistance, he'd found the burdens to be almost intolerable.

Something or someone was intruding.

"Excuse me, General Eng." The voice was persistent, breaking through the horror of his dream.

"What?" he gasped, as he sought to separate the real from the imagined.

"We are about to land, sir, and I thought you might like a hot towel and a cup of tea."

"I was dreaming...."

"Yes, general. Let me help you adjust your seating."

The general wondered whether his devoted servant had heard him cry out the truth, but it didn't matter. For the next two days, he was scheduled for a layover in San Fransisco. His lips—and any to whom he might speak—would be silenced soon enough.

The Interrogation

Deep River Junction, Vermont
April 22nd, 10:25 p.m.

The sheriff moved around the corner of the gutted house just as the man climbed stiffly from his car. The policeman's presence didn't register on him at all, but his emotional shell was cracked when he noticed three teams of stretcher-bearers staggering toward the ambulances through the steaming rubble. His eyes turned to follow them, and he faltered when he realized that the victim's heads were covered.

"Oh, my God," he groaned.

The sheriff had moved in beside him. "Do you...that is, did you," he corrected himself, "know the victims?"

The man seemed oblivious to the question as he turned to follow the EMS teams toward the ambulances, moving with the leaden steps of one trapped in a nightmare. The sheriff, weary from working a double shift and long inured to suffering, was unusually clumsy in his attempt to project a compassionate mien. He caught the man by the arm.

"Excuse me, sir," he said, barely civil, as he shined his flashlight full in his face. The intense beam caused him to avert painfully dilated eyes, but the cop persisted. "You were this woman's husband, the father of these children?"

"Were?" he croaked. The horror that he was trying to deny was now confirmed with these awful words of authority. He raised his eyes, but the light again dazzled him, intensifying his headache, and he cupped his open hand to shield them. "Were?" he repeated in a whisper, turning to survey the wreck of his home, the remains of his family.

The sheriff repeated his question.

After a moment, the man replied in resignation, "Yes. This is my family."

The policeman found himself offering a marginally sincere, "I'm sorry, sir." His words carried almost the right tone of professional interest, but the cadence with which he uttered them indicated little sincerity, even to his own jaded ears. Nevertheless, he found himself pressing remorselessly on. "Did you and your wife have just the two children, sir?"

Oh Lord, he thought, please, not both of them!

Yet even as he offered this silent prayer, his heart rebelled against the officer's callous questions. How could anyone, much less a sheriff, use the word, 'just,' when referring to children? What's more, these weren't just two children. These were his children, his flesh and blood, and this morning they had been living, breathing human beings.

Has human life become so cheap, he wondered. But discretion kept him from screaming the question, 'Are my children so meaningless to you?' His shoulders sagged as he choked back a rush of bile. It was strange how he seemed to be outside himself, as though he were watching himself handle this all so badly. Insignificant thoughts raced through his mind, preventing him from dealing with matters in any sort of orderly or logical fashion. He couldn't deal with the loss of his family with the same dispatch he would have exercised on his radio show when discussing someone else's pain. *Maybe I've become just as callous as this cop,* he thought. *No, that couldn't be so.*

This was different. This was intensely personal. He realized that he had to be careful. He was too close to this situation. Close? He was at its center. Apart from the fact that he'd just lost his wife and children, and that something within him had died with them, he sensed that something far larger, and far more ominous was taking shape around him. It wasn't simply that he'd lost his wife and children.

So even as he tried to grasp the enormity of his own loss, he was unconsciously processing other information. Up until now, he'd wanted to believe that all the reverses that had occurred in the past seventy-two hours had been coincidental —the loss of his radio program, the theft of his identity, the simultaneous emptying of his bank accounts, and the tapping out and cancelation of his credit cards—but now he was being told that his entire family had also perished. The likelihood of their dying in a fire, added to these other disasters, defied reason.

How could this have happened? He'd installed an excellent smoke detector system in his home, and he'd hung fire extinguishers in key places around the house. He and his wife had not only planned for escape from fire, but had actually conducted a couple of fire drills in the middle of the night. He turned to look at the ruins of his house. Obviously these efforts had been of no use at all.

So when the policeman started asking him questions, he grew angry. And he considered any attempt this policeman might make to turn this horror into some sort of theoretical discussion as something bordering on the blasphemous.

"The Lord giveth and the Lord taketh away," intoned the cop. Perhaps he meant well, but the sound of his voice seemed to ring with a terrible dissonance, and the man clenched his teeth and forced himself to remain silent.

As far as any discussion was concerned, the sheriff knew that he held an advantage. He'd already divined the man's identity and, if his talk radio persona was to be believed, he also realized that he was probably a pretty decent guy.

This fire, however, appeared to be the result of arson, and if it was arson, then it was homicide. Hence, he had to conduct a thorough investigation. And though he was sure that this man was probably innocent, and even believed that he shared many of his values, that was only an assumption based on what he'd heard of his radio programs, and not through personal acquaintance. He could just as well be a fraud and a hypocrite. Most celebrities, including Christians, were not what their publicists claimed.

As a cop, he had always tried to deal with all suspects in the same manner, reasoning that his approach would help him get to the truth of the matter. He had learned to speak and act in a certain manner simply because it had proven effective to do so. And though others might think he was unnecessarily cruel to suspects, he knew he needed to drill down in order to get the information he'd need to solve a case. If someone murdered this man's family, there had to be a reason, and even if this guy were as clean as the driven snow, he very likely had some information, some hidden clue, as to the guilty person's identity, though he might not realize it himself.

Unfortunately, although the suspect seemed to sense his intentions, he was also understandably angered by his behavior. It was clear to him that he'd gotten off on the wrong foot. Ostensibly the victim would be suffering terribly at the loss of his family, but apart for that, the sheriff had no knowledge of the other issues tearing at him. So while the policeman was in a very real sense trying to secure the information required in order to clear the man, the suspect saw it as painful and unnecessary meddling. And he had determined that this cop, who he initially considered a shallow excuse for a human being, would never be allowed to suspect how intensely he was moved by viewing these remains.

Tears nevertheless came unbidden to the man's eyes. He shook his head not so much to deny his pain as to clear his thoughts, but he couldn't hide his anger as he sarcastically choked out the sheriff's last baneful question. "Just the two children?" He turned his head to look over his shoulder at the cop's face. "Is that what you asked me? Just the two children?"

"I'm sorry, sir. I know that this may be difficult for you, but I must ask you a few questions."

"...may be difficult?" the man repeated with an acidic irony.

The sheriff ignored his comment and went blithely on, remorselessly ignoring the plea in the man's eyes, with what appeared to be the arrogance of petty authority.

Now the man focused on the officers name which was etched in a plastic plate pinned above his shirt pocket.

"Sheriff John McClaren."

Whoop de do! This guy's the boss. He was elected by, "We the people." Funny. We've lived in this rural town for years, but I've been home so rarely that I've met very few people. His mind wandered. *It seems to me that my wife campaigned for this bum. It would be easy to understand why he'd be behaving in this manner if he were only a poorly-trained deputy, but it's difficult to believe that a Sheriff would behave like this, especially in a lightly populated county like this. He's certainly aggressive.*

And, in fact, the cop seemed coldly indifferent to the look of antagonism that the man now wore as he raised his chin and pulled back his shoulders.

Even though the sheriff knew from long experience that such a suspect was particularly vulnerable at a moment like this, and that this was perhaps the ideal time to secure meaningful statements on which to build a case, he was impressed with this man's almost fearless indifference to his authority. He wasn't exhibiting the false bravado of a liar, yet the sheriff felt it necessary to persist a little longer, though he was beginning to regret that he was forcing his suspect to defer any personal sorrow.

"Are you the father?" he demanded.

This age of spiritual malaise also fostered the neglect, abuse, and murder of children, so law enforcement agencies had to be continually alert for evidence of possible mistreatment. Ironically, it was an age in which good parents were often legally harassed by incompetents who were improperly vested with too much authority. So while the sheriff was trying to do his job, his suspect was not ignorant of his devices. And although he was aware of the often illegal maneuvers made by some cops, his righteous indignation had spawned anger, and he had become careless of the consequences.

"Aren't you going to read me my rights?"

The sheriff stared keenly at him. This growing belligerence, when he had initially concluded that the suspect might be blinded by grief, now stiffened his own resolve. Was this a bluff? Would this guy back down if threatened?

"Do I need to read you your rights?" he asked evenly, wondering if their mutual hostility might simply be a matter of the burdens that were wearing on both of them.

The man, his face haggard, didn't bother to respond, but simply stared blankly at the ambulances.

In an effort to intimidate the man, the sheriff directed his flashlight onto a small spiral notebook and scribbled a few words, printing in large enough characters to make it easy for his suspect to read them over his shoulder. It proved an exercise in futility. Although he used his flashlight to illuminate the page, and provided the man with ample time to absorb what he'd written, the suspect never so much as glanced at the page.

It was at that moment that the Sheriff knew intuitively that the man wasn't guilty of any crime, much less murder. He flipped the notebook closed, then turned to reexamine him.

He was deeply troubled, of course, but he obviously wasn't concerned about being a suspect. At that moment, the sheriff realized that he didn't need to check whether Mr. Conservative Christian Talk Show Host had any kind of a record with Family Services, or anywhere else for that matter.

Of course the man looked terribly weary. It was obvious that he was barely able to stay awake in spite of the horrors he was experiencing—or maybe because of them. The cop couldn't know that his syndicated show had just been canceled, or that vicious attacks on his reputation had already put him under enormous stress. He had no idea of the depths of despair the man had reached.

He consulted his watch. "Can you tell me where you were earlier this evening, say about 7:30?" The man dragged his eyes away from the ambulances and studied him dully, as though trying to grasp what he was asking.

The sheriff repeated the question, and stiffened as the man's hand slid under the lapel of his suit coat, relaxing only when the hand that was withdrawn contained only a blue paper envelope. The suspect held it out to the sheriff without offering any explanation.

The sheriff took the envelope and flipped back the cover to discover an airline boarding pass. He closed the cover, and handed it back to the man. Albany's two hours away, he thought. Even if this guy drove above the speed limit and caught every green light, he couldn't have been anywhere near here when the fire started.

"Did you check any bags?"

The man raised his eyebrows, mildly surprised at the question. He pulled the boarding pass from the sheriff's fingers, flipped it over, and pointed to the baggage check stapled to the back.

That means, the sheriff concluded, that he would have had to wait at least another thirty minutes after landing just to claim his luggage, for although Albany was a small airport, baggage handling was often slow. As a result, the union baggage handlers at Albany were among the Sheriff's own pet peeves.

The suspect's actions were ingenuous. At the moment, he would never have imagined that anyone would have seriously considered him capable of any sort of crime, much less murdering his wife and children. So his thoughts were elsewhere.

The past few weeks had been fraught with problems. His

entire future had seemed in doubt, and he had flown home two days ahead of schedule to tell his wife that his long-term contract had suddenly and mysteriously been canceled, and that they were nearly broke. He had so looked forward to getting home to his family. To hold them. To pray with them. To try to laugh off their problems together. Instead, this! The sound of the rear doors of an ambulance being slammed arrested his attention. What am I going to do without you, was his mute cry.

During the flight home he'd buried his face in his hands, and presented his arguments to God in a pathetic parody of prayer, trying to justify himself—pleading that God do something for him.

He'd tried to contact the few men that he had considered his close friends and associates, but they were all unavailable. Yet, until he'd pulled his automobile up next to the smoking remains of his home, he had still clung desperately to the thought that the Lord had not for some reason forsaken him. The hope vanished when he saw the three bodies being carried toward the ambulances.

The loss of his job and the end of his career had seemed momentous, but they were of no consequence now. He laughed ruefully, and the sheriff turned toward him, wondering what he could possibly find funny, but the man didn't notice, for he suddenly felt as though his soul was a battlefield, his "old man" warring with the "new," and winning.

It's one thing for a preacher to mouth some high-sounding phrase like, "Though He slay me, yet will I trust Him," he thought, *but quite a different thing to live those phrases out while watching the bodies of his wife and children being carried away from the ruins of their home.*

Then it was as though he'd heard a disembodied voice

speak. "There has no temptation taken you but such as is common to man." Instead of being encouraged, he wanted to argue back, *That may be, but brother Job didn't have a thing on me.*

Again his maudlin meditations were interrupted, and the end of that verse came to mind. "God is faithful...He will make a way of escape that you will be able to bear it."

It's too late, he wanted to retort, *unless You are prepared to bring my wife and children back to life.* Tears trickled down his cheeks!

While he was involved with these painful introspections, the sheriff's thoughts were heading down a different avenue. He again turned to the man.

"Let me verify your ID please." Even that procedure had become a matter of form, a reflex action. It was a phrase every cop had uttered countless times, like a clerk asking "Paper or plastic?" or a stranger saying "Have a good day." Any courtesy had become a veneer that cloaked necessary formalities.

The Sheriff had decided that he didn't need to occupy the man further because he'd come to the conclusion that he was innocent. Nor did he need his ID, because he already knew who he was, though it always paid to follow the prescribed procedures. When he filled out his reports, he wanted to be absolutely certain that he'd crossed every t.

As the sheriff waited for the man to produce his driver's license, he noticed what he imagined to be the flare of a cigarette being lit among the trees in the vacant lot across the street. *Has the arsonist hung around to see his handiwork?* he wondered.

He started to turn toward the woods when several other things happened. First, the suspect held out his wallet, his thoughts far away. As he proffered the wallet, the sheriff grabbed for his chiming cell phone with one hand, while waving off the wallet with the other.

He turned his eyes to the buttons on his cell phone while mumbling to the suspect, "Remove your identification from the billfold, please."

The man, lost in his own thoughts, had released his grip on the wallet at the same instant that the officer had pushed his hand away, and the billfold had fallen unnoticed into the deep grass beneath their feet.

The Evasion

Deep River Junction, Vermont
April 22nd, 10:35 p.m.

The man stared vacantly toward the two firemen as they directed the spray from their nozzle over the smoking rubble that had been his home. When the sheriff's voice penetrated his ruminations, and he returned his attention to him, he realized that he wasn't speaking to him but to someone on his cell phone. As a matter of courtesy, he stepped back, only to find himself nearly enveloped in the singed branches of the evergreen that towered in the corner between what had been the two wings of his gutted house.

His mind drifted. It was as though he could hear his children's voices as they played beneath its boughs. He could hear them pleading with him as Christmas approached, to run lights up its entire thirty-foot height. His mind continued drifting until a bough scratched his face, bringing him back to reality.

The sheriff's phone conversation then captured his

attention. Although he was shrouded in semi-darkness, the policeman was dramatically illuminated by the glaring floodlights mounted atop the fire engines. As he studied the sheriff's face, and tried to follow his words, he realized that the officer was both angry and indignant.

"What do you mean, 'arrest him?'" he asked in apparent disbelief. "It's already obvious that he's an innocent victim."

It was, of course, impossible to hear the words of the caller, but the sheriff calmly answered the next question.

"No, he flew into Albany a few hours ago. He couldn't possibly have been here when the fire started. He has an airtight alibi."

While the traumatized man listened unbelieving to this one-way conversation between the sheriff and an unknown but obviously influential caller, it became more obvious that someone wanted his hide nailed to the wall. And as he strained to make out the words, he also realized that, while involved with the phone call, the sheriff appeared to be intentionally ignoring his own movements. He had even turned to face away.

The fact that the sheriff was ignoring him seemed as strange as the realization that the caller wanted him prosecuted for something he obviously hadn't done. Although he was standing several yards away, he was suddenly able to get the gist of the conversation because the sheriff had inexplicably turned on the phone's speaker and pumped up the volume. As he continued to eavesdrop, it became obvious that the sheriff was interceding on his behalf. What's more, he left no mystery about who was calling him.

"Look, Mr. Mayor," he said, now clearly angry, "I can't begin to imagine why you are involving yourself in the matter of a late night fire...." His voice trailed off as the caller interjected a comment.

"What's Shariah Law have to do with this?" he demanded. The voice on the other end had become shrill, but was still fairly indistinct.

"Yes, I know that the legislature has incorporated it into a proposed state law, but the governor hasn't signed that bill yet, and if he does, I'm sure it will be challenged in the courts."

Now there was an angry retort from the caller.

"What do you mean, the law is none of my business? Of course it's my business. I'm an officer of the court!" Then, another riposte, and the sheriff shouted back, "Don't threaten me!"

Although the man was standing ten feet away hidden in the branches of the old evergreen, it was obvious that he was the subject of their conversation. Since he could hear many of the mayor's words as they were amplified by the speaker phone, he no longer felt guilty for eavesdropping.

Why, he wondered, *did the sheriff turn on the phone's speaker?* There was certainly something strange going on here, and he was surprised that this sheriff, whom he had at first considered slovenly, seemed to possess deep convictions that were being severely tested as the argument with the mayor escalated.

The Sheriff was obviously determined to hold off his caller, and was mixing in constitutional arguments with exact quotes from the law. At one point he spoke in lay terms. "It's a fundamental rule of law, Mr Mayor. A person is considered innocent until proven guilty."

"Rule of law be damned," he heard the mayor shout. "The president has declared a state of emergency and invoked a number of executive orders that give him virtual dictatorial powers. What's more, we all know that the majority of the electorate support imprisoning terrorist suspects even if there is a lack of hard evidence to convict them. And, as I understand the situation, hundreds of suspects, like the man you have there, have already been taken into custody, and dozens have been shot while resisting arrest."

"Dozens shot to death? You're exaggerating!"

"Not a bit!" Then he added, the threat evident in his voice, "And many of those who sought to shield them from arrest were shot as well."

"You don't mean law enforcement officers?"

"I do." He seemed to take satisfaction in his next statement. "After all, policeman are subject to the law too, and you have gotten away with far too much for far too long."

It was obvious that the sheriff was struggling to restrain his anger. "Who is doing this shooting?"

"Well, it's really none of your business, but the president's executive orders are being enforced by select officers of the IRS, agents who have been thoroughly trained and equipped with the latest weaponry by Homeland Security. They in turn are supported by a large contingent of men and women who were rehabilitated while in state and federal prisons and are now assisting in keeping the peace."

The sheriff was clearly dumbfounded. It was several seconds before he could speak.

"The president is arming ex-convicts?"

"Of course. Why not? 'Set a thief to catch a thief,' so to speak."

"And these armed ex-convicts have already killed hundreds of people?"

"Yes, and if your attitude is typical, it's clear that they will be called upon to do much more."

The sheriff was rocked by his words, but at the same time strangely unsurprised. He thought, *It's like Nazi Germany, with their SS and the Gestapo. The inmates are now in charge of the prisons.*

After a moment of silence he asked, "What happened to *habeas corpus?* What happened to the *U.S. Constitution?*"

"Americans would rather feel safe than worry about someone else's dubious Constitutional rights," the mayor intoned piously, and the sheriff understood, to his sorrow, that it was probably true. The sheriff couldn't think of anything else to say, so he didn't pursue the issue. Instead, he asked, "What's your point?"

"My point is that, if you don't do your job, maybe you won't have your job."

"This all sounds like blackmail to me," rejoined the sheriff. "On the other hand, I guess I could live without this job, so again I'll ask, 'So what?'"

"So what? I'll tell you so what. We're authorized to detain anyone," and he repeated the word in an even louder voice, "anyone that we consider a potential threat."

"Who is the 'we' you're referring to? And what constitutes 'a potential threat,' and to whom? Are you talking about a potential threat to the nation, or to the president's dictatorial ambitions?" And before the mayor could respond, the sheriff followed with another question. "But getting back to my situation here, and apart from your seditionist rhetoric, how's this particular man that I've been questioning a threat to anyone?"

The mayor shouted, "It's none of your business!" Then he blustered, "I have information you don't have."

"What information?"

"Well, for one thing, he's a Christian millennialist."

"A Christian who believes that Christ will some day return and establish a thousand year reign on earth somehow represents a terror threat?"

"Absolutely."

"Let's examine that idea for a moment."

"Go right ahead."

"Christians who are serious enough about their faith to believe in the return of Christ tend to champion the Constitution. They are law-abiding, peaceful, patriotic, and stable. They have a strong work ethic, and a sense of independence. And they believe that government is best which governs least. They are generous, forgiving, and tend to mix well with other ethnic and national groups."

The mayor laughed. "There! You've put your finger on the problem."

"Huh?" The sheriff was speechless.

"Christians are inflexible, intemperate, and unable to accept change. They live in the past. They refuse to accept the findings of science, such as evolution and global warming, they oppose the most fundamental social changes, such as abortion and same-sex marriage, and they cling to the outdated Constitution while turning their backs on the inevitability of a one-world government. Surely you can see that Christianity has outlived its usefulness as a religion?"

The sheriff was stunned. *This discussion is going nowhere,* he concluded.

"Let's get back to the issue at hand. What did you mean when you said that this man's status is none of my business? I am, after all, the sheriff."

"Just temporarily," the mayor muttered.

"What did you say? 'Just temporarily?' You seem a bit confused, Mr. Mayor."

"What do you mean?"

"I mean that I don't work for you. Let me remind you that I am the duly elected county sheriff operating within the scope of my authority, and I answer only to the people who elected me." Then he added, "And, by the way, this house fire is not within city limits and therefore not within your jurisdiction."

"Well, the Secret Service is moving into this state under Presidential Executive Order, and they insist that their federal powers exceed your local authority."

"And I insist that their claims exceed their powers. It's an unconstitutional power grab. What's more, I will resist any effort by a national secret police force to operate in this jurisdiction," the sheriff replied evenly.

"Well we will soon see who's right!" the mayor snarled. "And whether you think you answer to me or not, you'd better do what I tell you, or you'll find that you've lost a lot more than your job. Then he added, "You need to think about the welfare of your family."

The sheriff was silent for a moment, just looking off into space, counting slowly to ten. He didn't make it.

"It almost sounded as though you were threatening the lives of my family."

The mayor moderated his tone. "Listen, sheriff. The man you have there is bad news. Just take my word for it, okay? Do what I say. Take him in and hold him for questioning until our people get there."

"And who are your people?"

"They'll present you with the appropriate credentials."

"All I'll say, Mr. Mayor, is that, in the interests of cooperation between county and city law enforcement agencies, I'll take your suggestion under advisement."

"You'd better do more than that," he returned, even if you don't understand why. You'd just better know that the man you have there has enemies in high places. And you really don't want to make those people your enemies as well."

"Here's what I understand. Too many Americans, for far too long, have been too ready and willing to surrender their authority and responsibility to a soulless government without understanding why, and their acquiescence, as much as anything, explains the sorry state of our nation today."

The mayor was bullying now. "You aren't listening, sheriff. You'd better do what I've said or you'd better find yourself a hole and crawl into it."

The sheriff wanted to say, I'*d be afraid it's the hole you crawled out of,* but he didn't. He instead said, "I'm curious. Do you count yourself among this man's enemies, mayor, or are you just sucking up to the people you think are going to take over America?"

"That's enough! You'd better get your mouth under control." Then the mayor realized he was shouting again, and made an effort to rein in his temper. "My relationship to these people isn't your concern. I do what they tell me. And you'd better too, if you know what's good for you."

"And what's that?"

"Put handcuffs on that guy, and take him in."

"What makes you think I have him in custody?"

"I know that you've been questioning him."

"How could you possibly know where I'm located, much

less that I'm questioning anyone, or who that someone might be?" The sheriff looked around, but all he saw were the emergency personnel doing their jobs. Then he again noticed the glow of a cigarette in the trees across the street. He returned his attention to his caller. "By the way, how did you even know there was a fire at this location?"

The man standing in the dark embrace of the evergreen was jolted by the question, and unconsciously pushed himself further back into the pine boughs. The tip of a stiff old broken branch pressed painfully into the small of his back, and when he twisted a little to his right to relieve the pressure, it slipped on past him, shielding him even further from the sheriff's view. Now, hidden in the pine boughs, he began searching the shadows around the house, trying to figure out whether the mayor might actually have someone spying on them. He too saw the sudden glow among the trees in the park across the street.

His attention was drawn back to the sheriff whose voice had taken on an incredulous tone. "You expect me to arrest this guy on the legal ground that he's a terrorist?"

He could no longer hear the mayor's words as clearly, but he could hear the sheriff's responses, and the sheriff seemed to be purposely directing his voice toward the tree where he had been standing moments before. "

"Yes, mayor, you did tell me that thousands of Americans are being picked up on the guise of being terrorists, but you and I both know that the federal government has actually been promoting terrorism for years. In fact," he went on, "our esteemed leaders have been encouraging and supporting illegal aliens, drug lords, foreign despots, and international terrorists, supplying them with housing, food stamps, medical care, cell phones, and even firearms. And it's no secret that, while that was going on, the IRS and other governmental agencies were harassing and arresting law-abiding citizens and seizing guns from those who held different political views. Yet all that notwithstanding, the man you are referring to is no more a terrorist than the man in the moon."

He could see the sheriff's face through the branches, and the cop looked like he wanted to throw his phone across the yard.

"You're wrong!" he heard him shout. "I think I have a pretty good idea of what's going on, and it looks to me like the president is attempting to stage a coup d'état."

A short harangue from the mayor followed, and then the sheriff had his say.

"Well, threatening to get me fired is one thing, but threatening to charge your county sheriff with terrorism because he questions the actions of an out-of-control government, or because he refuses to arrest an innocent man, is something else again."

The caller had lowered his voice, and the man hiding in the branches could no longer make out his words. Then the sheriff slumped in resignation, but a moment later seemed to regain stature as he squared his shoulders and raised his head. Unable to hold back his contempt, he asked in a quiet, almost menacing voice, "Okay, let's wrap this up. You're suggesting that he's an enemy combatant, and ordering me to jail him immediately?"

The sheriff paused for a moment, obviously listening to the voice at the other end. Then, raising his eyes, and staring pointedly into the darkness toward where the man was hidden, he said quite loudly, "Yes, Mr. Mayor. I am, to rephrase your illegal orders, confirming that you have overstepped your legal authority and have ordered me to jail this innocent man, charging him as a terrorist and an enemy combatant, and that, if he resists, we are to shoot him dead. Is that correct, Mr Mayor?"

There was no question in the man's mind that he was the "enemy combatant" under discussion in this incredible conversation, but his thinking was so muddled from the events of the past few days that he couldn't begin to reason out why all this was happening.

It was clear from this conversation that he did indeed have enemies in high places, and, on the basis of some of the things he'd said on his radio show, he supposed he could understand why some would consider him a threat to their political ambitions, especially a megalomaniac intent on taking over the country. It nevertheless staggered his imagination because he'd always considered himself relatively small potatoes in the world of those who shaped public opinion. Yet, if someone were attempting to overturn the government of the United States, they'd obviously go to any extreme to silence all opposing voices.

He shook his head. It didn't make sense. His syndicated show was off the air, so if the country was already in the throes of revolution, and in imminent danger of takeover, what point was there in having him arrested? And how could this be? The only reports he'd heard on the major news networks dealt with the stock market collapse, the banking crisis, runaway inflation, and the likelihood of war, but not with a potential political coup. Then he remembered that virtually all major media outlets had been in the hands of the leftists for years. Why, he thought, should I be surprised at being kept in ignorance by the press?

While he was examining these thoughts, the sheriff had remained rooted in place, seemingly staring through the darkness at him. During a particularly long harangue from the mayor, he'd waved his hand and jerked his head as if to say, "Get out of here!" Looking through the branches, the man couldn't be sure. The sheriff again turned completely around so that he was facing in the opposite direction.

O Lord, the man prayed, *what am I to do? Is he giving me the chance to leave?* Then he reasoned, *Why shouldn't I leave? The sheriff never said I was under arrest. In fact, he just told the mayor that he refused to arrest me. I've done nothing wrong, so I'd be a fool to hang around here.*

Now the sheriff was stretching out his arm toward him, using the phone like a pointer, and he was again able to hear the caller shouting. Then, while the caller was in mid sentence, the sheriff evidently pressed a button to mute the phone, and spoke directly to him. "You," he shouted, get out of here, quick. Run for your life!" Then he turned his back on him again, and he could hear the mayor shouting, "Sheriff, are you there?"

"Of course, I'm here." The sheriff brushed away a smoldering flake of newspaper that had drifted through the air and landed on the sleeve of his uniform blouse. Then his eyes tracked back to the pine tree where his suspect was no longer visible. "And let me tell you something. Whether you are an opportunist, or a starry-eyed idealist who has foolishly thrown in your lot with that crowd to help them in their rise to power, you may be in for a rude awakening when you learn that you are no longer needed."

"Just a minute!"

"No, you wait just a minute. Once they've gotten everything they can squeeze out of you, and you begin to realize that you made a mistake, they may decide that you have become a liability to them. Hitler and Stalin killed off tens of thousands just like you who initially helped them gain power."

The man half-hidden in the shrubbery was no longer paying attention to the conversation, but was now near panic. He'd been pressing back against the branches of the evergreen when he imagined that someone grabbed his shoulders from behind and yanked him backwards. His immediate reaction was to back peddle with his feet in order to keep from falling. He suddenly found himself on the opposite side of the tree, completely hidden from the sheriff's view, and when he looked around, it was clear that the person who'd pulled him clear around the tree had disappeared.

How, he wondered, *could anyone have touched me, and then gotten away without my seeing or hearing him? Yet I definitely felt someone grab my shoulders! I guess I'm just stressed out. Maybe I stumbled over a rock or something.*

He continued backing up until he found himself pressing against one of the less damaged walls of the house, filthy with water and soot. Crouching down, he duck-walked between the wall and a row of the overgrown shrubs until he'd slipped around the far corner of the house. He rose in the shadows, then looked back between the branches so that he was able see the sheriff still in animated conversation with the mayor.

Go back, or run for it? he wondered. *I haven't done anything wrong, and if I can avoid it, I'm not going to jail, certainly not to be stood before some kangaroo court.*

Once resolved in his determination to escape the scene, he walked quickly down the side of the house and turned another corner. Then forcing himself to walk slowly so as not to attract the attention of the firemen, he made his way across the street to his car.

Slipping behind the wheel, he pulled the door closed as

quietly as he could. Turning the key to start the engine, the familiar sound of the doors automatically locking went unnoticed. He leaned forward, weekend-calloused hands clenching the wheel, forehead pressed hard against its rim, trying to settle his muddled thoughts, and trying not to think of his wife and children.

"Oh, God!" he choked.

Caught up as he was in his sorrows, his attention was captured when the sheriff moved to his patrol car and inexplicably turned on the multicolored strobe lights mounted on the roof.

The man wondered why the sheriff had turned on the flashing lights. Then, inexplicably, he felt a sense of foreboding, a subconscious warning that was almost palpable, leaving him with a growing sense of terror. He reacted by jerking the gearshift into reverse, and pressing the gas peddle to the floor. The wheels spun and the car fishtailed as it bounced off the curb and raced backward down the street. A man leapt out of his way, and he thought about stopping to apologize until he noticed the ski mask pulled down over his face and a knife in his hand.

With that, he threw the shift into forward, spun the steering wheel, and raced down the street away from the house. Checking his rear view mirror, he glimpsed the man disappearing into the woods that lay across from the remains of his home. Then he heard a siren. Checking his rear view mirror, he realized that the sheriff wasn't pursuing him, but had turned his car around and was accelerating down the street toward the far side of the woods, evidently to head off the man on foot.

How much more of this can I take? he wondered. He sped down the street, then slid around a corner onto a narrow lane, hoping he would lose anyone who might be following him. He was shaking with excitement, his fatigue momentarily gone. He'd gone from sorrow, to fear, to rage in less than a minute. *Was the guy with the knife the arsonist who murdered my family?* he wondered. He started to put his foot to the brake, but decided he'd better leave that question to the sheriff. Then it hit him. The guy with the knife had probably murdered his family in a blundered attempt to kill him. And it was obvious that he still intended to do so.

He turned a corner and slowed to the speed limit. When he was sure that the street behind him was empty, he pulled into the parking lot of a closed convenience store, turned off his headlights, and slid down in the seat. The right rear tire had seemed a little mushy on that last turn. Had the assassin slashed it? He looked for an air pump near the darkened gas pumps, but saw none. He'd have to remember to check that tire.

He was now troubled with the question of what to do. He thought of his wife. He had tried to reach her the previous evening, shortly before he had learned that his program had been canceled. When no one answered, he figured he'd call back later. And when he did call back to tell her that she should expect him to arrive home two days early, he again got no answer on either the house or her mobile phone, but he didn't have time to leave a message because the airline was paging him to board his plane.

He couldn't avoid taking a mental inventory. His family was dead, his home destroyed, his career over, his life in danger, and the nation in turmoil. He didn't know what to do. It occurred to him that he might go to his sister-in-law's apartment. He had never been close to her, for though she and his wife were much alike in appearance, even to the sound of their voices, they were actually very different. His wife was a strictly Proverbs 31 woman, while his sister-in-law was so morally loose that someone had once called her a Jezebel.

On the other hand, he did like his brother-in-law. He was a hard working, easy going godly man who spent his Sunday mornings in church with his kids, and the afternoons watching football. He was a good family man who took his children camping, almost worshiped his wife, and seemed blind to her philandering.

His wife had frequently tried to talk sense to his sister-in-law, to remind her how much she had to lose through her betrayal of her family, but this only resulted in terrible arguments, and after the last fight, they hadn't talked for weeks. Now, however, he knew that he had to call her.

Letting the engine idle, and leaving the lights off, he reached for his cell phone, and punched a button to speed dial the seldom-used number. After the fourth ring, a disembodied voice advised him that, "No one is available to answer your call, but if you'll leave your name and number...." He disconnected before giving the machine time to recycle, then leaned back and closed his eyes.

When he opened them a few minutes later, he noticed that it had begun to rain. A car's tires made whirring sounds as it passed by, its headlights glaring through his spattered windshield. Momentarily blinded by the light, he again closed his eyes and leaned his head against the cold damp glass of the driver's door. He sat like that for several minutes, then pulled himself erect, and slipped the transmission into gear. It would take about five minutes to get to his sister-in-law's home.

He walked into the hallway of the apartment building only to discover a man, obviously drunk, hammering on his sister-in-law's door. A frowsy woman, dressed in a chintz bathrobe, stood in an open doorway down the hall, shouting at the man to come home. The guy uttered a few profanities, then staggered back down the hall, whereupon the woman dragged him into her apartment and slammed the door.

After they were gone, he knocked lightly on the door. When he received no answer, he called softly, "Please, answer the door. Our house burned down." Choking on his words, and near tears, he raised his voice. "Chris and the kids were in a fire." He was nearly crying now, but there was still no reply to his knocking. Finally, with the woman down the hall again standing in her doorway watching him, he turned and left the building.

The Preppers

Deep River Junction, Vermont
April 22nd, 10:55 p.m.

By the time the sheriff had ended his call with the mayor, he knew without doubt that the man he'd been interrogating was a victim, not a perpetrator. And not simply a victim, but a political target.

During the course of the bitter exchange, he'd been keeping an eye out for his former suspect. He'd done everything but stand on his head to signal to the guy that he should run for his life, but he was unable to see him after he'd disappeared behind the big spruce.

He'd finally noticed him getting into his car, but then became concerned because the guy simply sat behind the wheel, doing nothing. He hadn't driven away, and that worried the sheriff who knew that there was nothing for him there but more trouble. And something didn't seem right to the sheriff. After nearly two decades at his job, it was as though he could smell more trouble brewing.

He'd wanted this guy to move on, but he didn't want to draw additional attention to the victim or to himself. He decided to try to spook him, and maybe shake the real perp loose, so he turned on the red and blue strobe lights on the roof of his patrol car. It had precipitated instant action on the part of the man, but not for the reason he'd expected. Out of the woods, running directly for the passenger door of the victim's parked car, raced a figure in dark clothes, knit ski cap pulled down over his face. It looked like he intended to open the door, but his hand slipped off the handle as the car suddenly lurched backward away from him.

The sheriff immediately slammed his own car into reverse, and with wheels spinning, backed around to pursue the masked assailant. At the same time, the victim completed a U-turn and succeeded in pulling away, whereupon the man in the stocking mask turned and ran toward the woods.

That's my arsonist, the sheriff concluded, and spun his car in a circle, hoping to catch the man on foot. But before he could catch him, he'd disappeared into the cover of the trees. The sheriff gunned his engine, continued down the street and took the corner on two wheels, hoping to reach the arsonist before he got back to his car. Again, he was too late. He heard the screech of spinning tires around the next corner, but by the time he reached the turn, the suspect had sped out of sight.

As he raced futilely in the general direction the killer had taken, he wondered whether the guy was in league with the mayor or some other group of conspirators. The way things had been going, he might even be a rogue agent of the government. It would certainly explain the mayor's real time knowledge of what was occurring at the crime scene. What frightened the sheriff was that, whoever "they" were, they'd had the time, resources, and especially the confidence to murder a man's family, then hang around to try to kill the survivor while he was being questioned by a law enforcement agent.

The sheriff's mind was racing. *It's understandable that fanatic radicals would stoop to murder in order to still their enemy's voices and gain power. For such people, the end justifies the means. Anything goes! Yet, the fellow travelers, those unwitting dupes and so-called idealists, often naively believe that they are somehow immune to such treatment.*

It's ironic that the idealistic left—from political pundits to media moguls—foolishly believe they will be rewarded for their efforts. History reveals that most political revolutions end with some strong man—a Stalin or a Hitler—rising from the gutter, then cementing his control by killing off his starry-eyed followers before they become disillusioned and attempt to expose him.

That's exactly what the Nazis did during their "Night of the Long Knives," he mused, *when they systematically murdered hundreds of Germans, not simply prominent anti-Nazis, but also members of their own party, including the brutal Brown Shirts who helped them attain their power.* "Is tonight another night of the long knives?" the sheriff wondered aloud. *It's pretty clear that someone was willing to murder an entire family just to get to this one man.*

Then he remembered that the mayor had just threatened

him as well, and it was suddenly clear that it was not an empty threat.

The sheriff flicked a button on the dashboard and the flashing lights on the roof went dark. Even if I caught the arsonist, he realized, his friends would get him off. And, besides, I've got more important things to do.

He returned to the site of the burned house and was stepping out of his patrol car when the fire inspector approached him.

"Well, sheriff, you were right. It's definitely arson, but we won't have the formal lab reports back from the FBI lab for several days."

The sheriff's only response were raised eyebrows.

"Gas explosion. It moved the walls off the foundation."

"So?"

"This neighborhood has all-electric houses. I checked. There are no gas appliances in this house. And take a look at this." He led the way around the corner of the house, and pointed down into a basement window well. A twenty-pound propane tank, like those used to operate gas grills, lay on it side next to the broken window. The fire inspector knelt down and drew a length of charred hose out of the cellar window. "Someone set this tank here, stuck the hose into the basement, and turned on the gas. I suspect we'll find some sort of simple timed fuse under the refuse in the basement that the arsonist dropped through the window to set off an explosion after enough of the highly explosive gas had filled the house."

The sheriff nodded his understanding.

"Thanks, Tom."

The fireman shook his head. "I saw you chasing someone down the street as I was pulling in. The killer?"

"I think so."

"It's typical of an arsonist to return to the scene to watch his work." He looked over his shoulder. "If he was hiding in those woods, watching the guys douse the fruit of his labors, your flashing lights should have scared him away."

"Yeah," the cop responded wryly. He turned toward the woods. "There was someone over there."

The fireman abruptly changed the subject. "I have a feeling we're not going to see you in church Sunday, Michael?"

"You're right about that. Danni and I have been thinking of getting away for a few days."

"Funny you should say that. A couple of the boys at the firehouse asked my opinion, and I flat out told them that it might be smart to leave town for a while." He pushed the toe of his rubber boot into the wet grass, then looked up under bushy brows. "You think so too, huh?"

"Nothing definite, Tom, but, yes, I think something's up. If you have any vacation saved up, it might be a good time to head for the hills."

The man's face tightened. "Okay, gotcha! I think I'll go home and gather up the family." As he turned to walk to his car, he looked back over his shoulder. "Thanks, buddy. And God bless!"

The sheriff nodded, then turned to query another of the firemen. "Did you see where that guy went?"

"What guy? The inspector?"

"No, the guy who was wandering around in the woods over there."

"Come on, sheriff," he said, clearly exasperated. "Can't you see we're busy here? I wasn't gazing off into any woods."

"Yeah, of course," the sheriff replied. "Sorry."

As he turned back toward his car, he took out his cell phone and punched in the mayor's speed dial. He ignored the angry sputtering from the other end, and waited for an opportunity to explain that the suspect had evidently escaped in the darkness during their earlier call, was being chased by another unknown individual, and that he'd been unable to ID either of them.

He detected a subtle lessening of tension when the mayor understood that an unknown individual was pursuing the home owner. In fact, the mayor was so satisfied with the turn of events that he suggested that the sheriff could terminate his own investigation. Then the mayor went on to use some of the very arguments on behalf of the homeowner that the sheriff had earlier used on him. "So, as you can see, sheriff," he concluded, "there's no real point in pursuing him further."

"Yes, Mr. Mayor," wondering if the forced tolerance in his voice was obvious to the other man. Then he asked, "But what about the guy pursuing him? Don't you imagine he might be the arsonist?"

"Hardly likely. Why would a criminal risk capture by returning to the scene of his crime?"

Why indeed, the cop wanted to pursue, but instead asked, "Why do you think he's chasing the other man?"

"Oh, it might be a family member or friend who came on the site just as he was leaving, and decided to try to catch up with him."

The sheriff listened to this with something akin to awe. *The mayor is a slimy guy, but you have to hand it to him; he really knows how to spin an argument.*

Then the mayor took another turn. "Just to play it safe, why don't you put out an all-points on the homeowner?"

"Can't do that unless he's suspected of a crime."

"Sure. Well, we don't really know he's innocent, do we? I mean, he took off about ten minutes ago, and the guilty man flees when no man pursues him."

This guy dares quote scripture? Then he asked himself, *How could he know when the homeowner had left the scene, unless someone had told him?* "How do you know he left here ten minutes ago?"

The mayor ignored the question, changing the subject, and the sheriff was forced to listen to his rant for a full minute before simply shouting into the phone, "Okay, I'll have an all-points put out on the owner of this home as soon as I get back to the station," and he terminated the call while the mayor was in the middle of a sentence.

He smiled grimly. I have no intention of returning to the station tonight because I feel I am at risk of contracting a serious fatal illness, such as a bullet or a knife in the back. So I'm going to call my wife and instruct her to call the office and notify the deputy on duty that I am taking a couple of days off.

As he was concluding the phone call to his wife, another fireman, who had been politely waiting a few yards away, came over to him with a muddy wallet in his hand. "I guess you must have dropped this, Sheriff."

"Thank you!" he replied. I must have lost it when I was looking around. Is the money still in it?"

"To be honest, Sheriff, I didn't look."

"Well, thanks." The sheriff commended him for his honesty, then wandered over toward the smoldering wreckage. Looking around to make certain he wasn't being watched, he removed the cash, credit cards, and identification, stuffed it in a pocket, then dropped the wallet to the ground. He took another look around, then kicked it through a broken basement window where it landed amongst a heap of glowing embers. After a moment, it began to smolder, then burst into flame.

As he turned away, he was startled by another figure watching him from the hedges. He was relieved to see that it was the town's fire chief.

"Well, sheriff—said the fire chief with just a touch of smugness—it looks like it's been a profitable night for both of us."

"Thank God, it's you!"

"What's with the wallet?"

"The guy who owns the house dropped it. The mayor wants him arrested, but as far as I'm concerned he's as clean as the driven snow."

"You bet he is. I may even know more about the situation than you do. Some very powerful people want that guy's head."

"I figured as much," the cop said, "so when I was handed the wallet just now, I decided to make certain that nothing in it could be used to locate the guy." Then he added, somewhat defensively, "I didn't know whether to hold on to the cash on the chance I'd run into him again, or drop it in the church offering plate."

"Well," the fire chief ran his fingers through his thinning hair, "I don't think you're going to have an opportunity to attend church this week."

"Why not? And, while I'm asking questions, why weren't you here fighting the fire with your boys."

"Because I was busy discovering that you've been right all along."

The sheriff raised his shaggy eyebrows in question. "So, you've seen the light?"

"You could say that, Michael. And, to use the vernacular, it's really hitting the fan."

"Could you be a little more specific, please? And maybe stop mixing your metaphors. What's hitting the fan?"

"The 'you-know-what' is hitting the fan. I've been busy trying to surf the Web."

"Trying?"

"Yeah, trying, John. There's not much web left to surf."

"What do you mean?"

"My ISP is still on line, but millions of sites are down, including all of those 'nutty conspiracy sites' that I was once skeptical of. In fact," he continued, "all the news sites and all the social sites are down. More importantly, all the banks are down. And most significantly, I couldn't find any government, military, or emergency preparedness sites either. And," he added, "It's virtually impossible to communicate via email."

"What about the remaining web sites you mentioned?"

The fire chief understood exactly what he was alluding to. "Several of the radical Islamic sites are still up," he answered, "and interestingly enough, they all have exactly the same home page, and they have only one line of text."

"And that line of text is...?"

"Two words," the fire chief replied with a frown. 'Allah Akbar.'"

"Jesus!" the cop uttered.

"No, not Jesus," he responded, tongue in cheek. "Allah Akbar mean, 'God is Great' or 'God is the Greatest.' It's one of the reasons that Muslims do not believe Jesus is God Incarnate. If he were God, he couldn't have died on the cross simply because 'God is Great.' And if God is the Greatest, He would never have a flesh and blood son, and even if he did, he wouldn't have sent him be put to death on a cross by mere human beings." He shrugged. "Anyway, that's their reasoning."

He and the fire chief had been close friends for many years, but sometimes the sheriff grew weary with his friend's tendency to pontificate. "The point, John. Get to the point!"

"That two-word phrase is called the Takbir, and it's one of the most significant utterances in Islam."

"Yes, I know that too," replied the sheriff. "And I know that it's so important that it's used in their prayers, on the flags of some of the countries they rule, and in some of their national anthems..."

"...and," added the fire chief, "it's shouted by Muslims engaged in Jihad."

"Holy war," finished the sheriff. "And those are the words on all the Islamic websites?"

"On all the sites that are still up. A couple of Islamic sites had been pleading for peace and conciliation, but they were either taken down or taken over."

"And all the remaining Islamic sites have those words?"

"Yeah, almost like a coded phrase instructing their followers, 'Loose the dogs of war!' And every Islamic website I checked was mirroring the same home page, a pale blue background with those two words printed in flaming characters.

"And your conclusions from this odd situation?" the sheriff pursued.

"Impossible to tell. Even though the operators of many of those sites might have opposed jihad, it's clear that the radicals, like Al Qaeda, have somehow taken control and posted their own message there. Oh, and there's more. Apart from the terrorist threat, there's something else of grave concern."

"And that is?"

Either someone at the top of our government is attempting to turn our once great republic into a dictatorship, or one or more enemy powers are about to attack us, or..." and he shook his head, "maybe all of the above." He hesitated. "One thing we know. There are over twenty million illegals from all over the world living in the good old U.S. of A, and not a few of them are well-trained, well-armed terrorists intent on tearing down our society."

"So, old friend," the sheriff asked, "how do you see that information impacting our professional responsibilities?"

"You mean you and me personally?"

"Exactly."

"Well, I see someone—our Islamic marxist mayor for example—ordering us into a situation that would be quite dangerous to our personal well-being."

"Yes, but isn't that what we signed on for," challenged the sheriff.

"We signed on to protect the people, not to die in some contrived disaster that will leave the bad guys in power and leave our citizens helpless victims."

"Interesting viewpoint," observed the sheriff.

"Especially when you realize that most of those in our community whom we once regarded as patriotic Americans have been beguiled into believing that those, like our esteemed mayor, have a better plan for the future of the good old U.S. of A," replied the fire chief.

"And your action plan?" the sheriff asked.

"I feel that the fire chief and the sheriff of this county are helpless to effectively assist the people at this time, and that they need to execute their long standing evacuation plan in order to save their own families."

"So you don't believe this is a false alarm, or," and the sheriff bit off the words, "cowardice in the face of the enemy?"

"No, I don't," the fire chief replied reasonably. "You see, there's something else I haven't told you."

"Which is?"

"According to some blogs I saw, people all over America, that is, military personnel, police officers, state troopers, fire chiefs, national guard officers, and especially county sheriffs—people like you and me—are being arrested and placed in detention camps."

"If that's true..."

"I even heard of a sheriff in New Mexico who has deputized everyone in his county to hold back a flood of heavily armed illegals coming up from the south."

"And," the sheriff pursued.

"He's been arrested by the secret service for sedition."

"It sounds like civil war."

"Worse!"

"Worse? How so?"

"World war."

The sheriff took a moment to respond. "How do you make world war out of this?"

"If you've been keeping up with the news, the heads of foreign governments, like France and Germany, have become increasingly angry and outspoken about the NSA's spying on them."

"And?"

"And they've concluded that our president isn't simply ambitious to rule America, but perhaps the entire world."

"That would explain a lot of things," the sheriff mused, "but it doesn't change anything for us."

"What do you mean?"

"At best, we're helpless to do any good here. At worst, we are in grave danger. So our best hope is to try to survive to fight another day."

"And how will we identify another day?" the fireman asked.

"You've got a lot of questions tonight," the sheriff answered, "and we don't have a lot of time, but I'll answer this one. In my opinion, another day is when we are able to differentiate between the bad guys and the good guys, and maybe join hands with those of like precious faith to fight back."

"Which is what we agreed on long ago, when we weren't sure that those conspiracy theorists were right, and when most people were condemning their thinking as insane."

"Yes. Regrettably, it seems that some of them were right."

"Regrettably, it looks as though life as we know it may be ending."

"Afraid so," the sheriff agreed.

"So, what's next?"

"Well," the sheriff replied, "I was just about to walk over to your fire engine and put my cell phone in the glove compartment."

"Sounds like an excellent idea," agreed the fire chief. "I

love my smart phone's GPS capabilities, and the way it helps me find my way around. But I don't like the fact that nasty people can determine my exact location. And I don't like the fact that those same people can listen in to my conversations without my knowledge or consent," the chief concluded.

"Bet you didn't know that they can track you, and even listen in on your conversations, even with your phone is turned off," the sheriff said.

"Not really!" the chief laughed in unbelief.

"Yes, really!" countered the sheriff. "You can be listened in on unless you remove the battery from the phone."

"But my battery's sealed in; I can't remove it," replied the chief.

"Exactly. And that's why both of our phones should go in the glove compartment. That way, anyone who tries to follow us by using our phone's built-in GPS systems will be tracking the fire truck, not us."

"Wonderful idea," agreed the sheriff, "but how do you know they haven't been listening to this conversation?"

The chief looked uncomfortable. "Well, to tell the truth, I don't. That was stupid of me."

"Stupid of both of us. So we'd better get a move on, don't you think?"

"Absolutely."

When the chief returned, the sheriff was digging through his pockets. "Ah, here it is."

There was curiosity in the chief's stare.

"Now that you've disposed of our phones, I will take this cheap little cell phone, which I registered under an assumed identity, and I will push this speed dial button for a conference call, and, as pre-arranged, I will address both of our wives at the same time, and I will not identify myself, but I will simply say, "My dog has run away from home."

The fire chief chuckled. "And how will they respond?"

"They won't say much," the sheriff answered in a sober voice. "They might simply say, 'I'm sorry to hear that.' Then they will hang up, gather up our children—along with miscellaneous cats, dogs, backpacks, and Bibles—get them all into their cars, and meet us at the diner on the edge of town for a quick late night snack...."

"...after which," the chief concluded, "we will all head for our little well-stocked hideaway in the mountains."

"Exactly, our little hideaway with the underground shelter."

"I'm glad we understand one another so well," the sheriff commented laconically.

"You know something?" the fireman asked, a broad smile on his face.

"What?"

"You look absolutely terrible."

"I guess it's knowing that our nation is in terrible trouble."

The fire chief grimaced. "Yeah, I feel terrible too." Then his optimistic nature bubbled to the surface. "Do you think I need a vacation?"

The policeman turned to him, barely able to hide his tears. "I think we both need a vacation. Let's get out of here."

The Mountain Road

Deep River Junction, Vermont
April 23rd, 2:08 a.m.

The mountains that rose about him were rendered invisible by the blowing snow of a late night spring storm.

In those dark pre-dawn hours, his world had diminished until it comprised only the upper curve of his steering wheel. The hacking of the wiper arms was made almost hypnotic by their pendulous swings and their metronome-like swish-swish. The road seemed fixed in the smeared zone of the windshield, a black polygon caught in the beam of his headlights, fuzzy with falling snow,

His entire benumbed world had become a small patch of highway whiting with snow, and the black arc of a steering wheel clenched in rigid hands, all framed in an ebony cloud of despair. He was in a tunnel, and the mouth of that tunnel appeared to be receding.

He was not conscious of the fact that the phenomenon he was experiencing is common to those in shock, that they become incapable of reason, and that the constriction of the blood vessels in the eyes may even cause the victim to lose his peripheral vision. As he stared disinterestedly down that narrowing optical tunnel, the movements that guided his vehicle around the perilous curves had become mechanical, controlled by habits developed through long years of driving.

If he had been able to move outside his tiny world of despair, he would have discovered that the sky hung too close to the earth, and that the glare and darkness discolored and distorted even the dangerously small area that he might have been able to see.

On the right side of the road the mountainside merged

with a steely-watered stream that was swollen with the melting snow, foaming and roaring as it tore down the mountain toward Deep River Junction. The raging stream occasionally dashed through a steel culvert beneath the pavement, as it passed beneath the highway from one side to the other. Stunted trees fought to root themselves in this blasted land, a roadway laid waste by builders widening the highway to satisfy the skier's lust to reach the slopes above. Since the highway was under construction, its dangerous switchbacks were marked only by snow-encrusted signs and tumbled orange barrels, their fluorescence blackened in the murk.

If the driver had recognized the dangers, he would not have cared, for he was terribly preoccupied. Little scenes from the past two days played out in his thoughts, then slid rapidly away to be replaced by others like some bizarre slide show. At first, his brain protected him by somehow numbing his thoughts. Then he was ruled by revulsion.

As the minutes passed, he was unable to shut out the reality of his wife's death and the vision of his children's bodies being carried toward the ambulances. The realization that someone had probably murdered his family in an attempt to kill him brought with it both an awful sense of shame for his having put them in such danger, and an implacable hatred that grasped him so violently that he could scarcely breath.

He wondered whether he was close to a heart attack when, inexplicably, a reassuring voice seemed to come out of nowhere. It provided a momentary sense of peace. He didn't want peace, however, but retribution. He relished his anger, and sought to override that voice. Full of hatred, he wanted revenge—to retaliate and to kill. He had no specific target, but if he did....

Fatigue added to his pain-filled confusion, yet his racing visions would not leave him. He added foul spices of his own to the dish of depression he was concocting. Inexplicably, he wondered whether his face reflected his bitterness. He adjusted the rear view mirror. The dark image that stared back at him was barely illuminated by the dash lights.

He expected to see a death mask. Instead, the familiar countenance that met his critical stare looked terribly weary, but not warped. His was certainly not a movie star's face, just the standard oval, with wide mouth, aquiline nose, a spray of wrinkles around light blue eyes, and framed above with light wavy hair. It was, he knew, all set above a medium height, medium weight frame. Kind of humdrum, he concluded, making it fairly easy for him to pass unnoticed in a crowd.

He had always believed that, with God's help, he could become whatever his mind could imagine, and the success he'd enjoyed as a result of his prayerfully determined efforts seemed for a while to bear out that conviction. Average appearance notwithstanding, he had a lot more going for him than the typical talking heads that read their carefully edited reports each evening on network TV.

He'd achieved notable success in broadcasting because his audience sensed that he not only blended knowledge with integrity, but that he had a sincere concern for them. Those listeners, after all, were sensitive to voice quality and the message content, but if they could actually see the speaker, their judgment might change.

He was a pretty square guy, and though sometimes tempted, he did not subscribe to Shakespeare's fatalistic view that "Life's but...a poor player that struts and frets his hour upon the stage and then is heard no more...." *It's certainly not "...a tale told by an idiot, full of sound and fury, signifying nothing."* Now, in spite of his earlier success, his convictions were being tested, for he'd run head-on into opposition that forcefully reminded him that there really is incredible evil at work in the world.

His brief self-appraisal had, for a moment, allowed him to exit his world of despair. It helped calm him, if only for a moment. There was no question in his own mind that, while outwardly unchanged, his inward man was altered forever.

He was emotionally exhausted, and had begun using the steel guard rail as a visual guide to keep him in his lane, but somehow it had become a leaden ribbon, dragging him remorselessly back into the bowels of despair. He had relived his experience at the scene of the fire over and over, and he was wracked with the twin trauma of heartache and headache.

How did it all come to this? he wondered.

Whitkowski Mushroom Caves

Lake Katrine, NY
April 23rd, 2:09 a.m.

The night before the attacks began, Jonathan Whitkowski had spent hours searching the web. His father and he hadn't been getting along very well for quite some time, and at about eight in the evening the senior Whitkowski opened his bedroom door and yelled at him to turn off the lights.

"If you're not going to the prayer meeting with us, then you're going to bed," he declared.

Jonathan and his father had been arguing over how much freedom a boy of his age should enjoy. Jonathan believed that he'd reached the age where he had a right to complete independence. His father retorted that freedom is not related so much to age as to maturity and godly behavior. "What's more," he declared, "there is no such thing as total independence." He went on trying to explain to seemingly deaf ears that independence requires commensurate individual responsibility.

"You will have to become accountable for your actions, and be more faithful in bearing your responsibilities."

As soon as his father and mother had left for church, he'd thrown back the covers of his bed and moved, fully clothed, to his bedroom window. He stood watching until he saw the tail lights on their pickup truck fade as they moved down the two lane state highway. Then he sat down at his computer.

Most attacks on sites in North America were now coming in from rogue regimes in nations outside the United States. For example, Jonathan knew of one small company whose server was cracked from North Korea. It's hard to know whether North Korea was actually the source of the attack, or if someone, somewhere else, was simply using a North Korean server as a proxy.

China too had been stepping up its already massive attacks. Some security professionals believed that China had long been operating the largest state-funded cyber-warfare operation. What was frightening about it were the rumors that the Chinese communists were working in conjunction with agents of America's NSA. Worse, China didn't just attack the defense and intelligence operations of other nations, but also exploited private corporation databases to gather information that could be used to attack core institutions such as financial, energy, transportation, and every critical aspect of the infrastructure, public or private, among all potential economic and military rivals, but particularly the United States.

On the night of the prayer meeting, none of Jonathan's fears about being apprehended mattered any longer. He was frightened because the number of successful attacks had increased an incredible tenfold over the past two days. Most of those attacks seemed to point back to China, the Middle East, and Russia, and were aimed at sites operated by the Department of Defense, as well as major financial institutions, airlines, railways, bridge and tunnel operators, and electrical generation and petroleum producers and distributers.

In other words, one or more nations, acting in concert, were successfully attacking and taking down website after website. In some cases, instead of shutting the sites down, they were actually taking control of them, and altering content. In the case of corporate and industrial sites, such as electrical generation and distribution, they were dictating from remote locations how much electricity was generated, and over what transmission lines it was moving.

It was obvious that America's enemies had learned to successfully penetrate and crash vital DoD websites as well. The government's alarm at the effectiveness of these attacks was made clear through the messages that were being exchanged, many in the clear, between members of various defense establishments and the Department of Homeland Security. It was so blatant that Jonathan realized that war must be imminent.

The danger of being discovered and tracked down for hacking was now extremely remote. On the other hand, there was no point in attempting it. The handwriting was on the wall. He could discover most of what he needed to know simply by surfing what remained of the web. When he visited sites operated by the various news outlets, he observed anchors and commentators expressing panic at the collapse of America's financial markets.

The information he gleaned caused him to realize that conditions were much worse than he'd imagined. One thing was certain. War was imminent. Jonathan came to the conclusion that missiles could be criss-crossing the skies at any moment. Worse, the attacks would likely be on a worldwide scale, with most aimed at the United States.

Jonathan envisioned the combatants as a group of bullies in a schoolyard at recess, ganging up on one lone kid. The only thing he couldn't figure out was whether America's adversaries were working together, or it was simply an opportunistic coincidence.

The Accident

Deep River, Vermont
April 23rd, 2:12 a.m.

He had cut and run from Deep River Junction with no special destination in mind, just a need to preserve what little of his life he still possessed. He'd lost everything—career, possessions, and family. Now he simply wanted to escape, to find a hole to crawl into so that he could lick his wounds.

The light rain had changed to snow as he'd left the town behind, and the vast mountain panorama which had stretched in snow-covered magnificence around the town was now lost in the darkness of a late winter storm. It was a world of death as well as a world of beauty. Yet he was indifferent to both.

The sound and heat of the blower had an anesthetizing effect, and as the increasingly heavy flakes caught the glass, they seemed to mask what little vision remained in his mind. It all seemed so peaceful. Almost catatonic, he leaned forward and shut off the wipers so that the windshield, and his memory, might become totally opaque. He would flee the scene which he had been replaying in his mind, just as he had fled it in his flesh.

He wanted someone else to deal with it, to somehow resolve it, so that things would return to the way they had been, without any memory of the horror of these past two days. He choked back the acid that rose in his throat, and idly mused that perhaps there could be a new life ahead, even a better life. Or perhaps life after death, though only the last of these seemed to offer any hope.

It occurred to him that he should try to pray. Chris would have wanted him to pray, to think positively, to trust the Lord. But he couldn't. At least not yet. He had always found it easier to pray for others than for himself. Many had even ascribed their own happiness to what they considered his wise counsel. He laughed ironically as the oft quoted words came back to him, "He saved others," they'd mocked Jesus, "himself he cannot save." The words, of course, referred to Jesus at the time of his crucifixion. But the words somehow seemed fitting in this situation as well. Then he immediately derided himself for comparing his misfortunes, no matter how severe, with the sufferings to which the Lord Jesus had submitted himself in order to provide salvation for the human race.

And yet with that thought, he realized that he couldn't just give up and let everything go. Leaning forward to turn the wipers back on, his mind began to race. This self-awareness, this reawakening hadn't risen out of his own being. Thinking of the suffering that Jesus Christ had experienced on his behalf was the beginning, but a *dunamis*, a supernatural power apart from his own reasoning had to be working within him.

He was led to think of the personal reappraisal that must lie ahead. He would have to follow the inevitable twists and turns of his inflamed conscience and tortured mind if he were to honestly resolve the hatred and confusion that threatened to overwhelm him. Just maybe I can get through this, he thought. He began to recite aloud, "The Lord is my shepherd, I shall not want...." His thoughts seemed to become clearer, more focused, and he again thought of his wife and children.

God has them now, he thought. Chris gave so much, suffered so much for our ministry, and we'd experienced so much financial stress. Funny! She'd never been able to enjoy the things most other women take for granted, but she didn't find her happiness in possessing things. Where many were grasping, she was giving, but it was clear that she never became bitter.

She gave the children the things that really mattered. The irony is that, after all her personal sacrifices, she was occasionally mocked by others who called themselves Christian ministers simply because they were rich in the things of this world. He admitted the truth to himself. *Once in a while I was jealous of their success, but we both knew that the Lord would take care of us, though it sometimes seemed unfair to me.*

As he thought back, he again acknowledged that God had always provided the essentials. *And isn't that exactly what He promised? "Give us this day our daily bread," and "My God shall provide all of your needs."* And he seemed to hear a voice say, "No greater love hath any man than this, that he lay down his life for another." *Okay,* he thought, *but why me? Why my wife and children?* And his eyes welled with tears so that he could scarcely see the windshield.

What am I doing out here in the middle of this storm? I've got to turn around. I've lost my family, but God has kept me alive. He must have some further purpose for my life.

He heard the wipers as they dragged across the crusted ice building up on the windshield. The blades were pushing the loose snow aside, but leaving behind an opaque frosted surface. He was suddenly frightened. How long since he had last seen the highway in front of him? An experienced driver becomes sensitive to the slightest change in an engine's sound, or a minor vibration in a car's ride. As he began to gently apply the brakes, he realized it was already too late.

He felt the tires slip, almost imperceptibly, on some unseen irregularity in the road, perhaps because of that spongy rear tire. He firmed his grip and let the car continue in the direction of the slide, gently pumping the brakes, hoping to forestall a more serious skid. The car began to slew sideways, and he pulled the wheel gently in the direction of the skid, hoping to gain sufficient traction to correct, but when he tried to edge it gently back, the tires broke completely free of the surface.

He peered through the small area of glass that had been cleared by the roaring defrosters. He could see enough to know that it was too late for him to do anything but hang on to the wheel and pray. The car seemed to accelerate as it slid across the unprotected shoulder toward the rocky bank of the roaring stream.

Burlington International Airport

Burlington, VT
April 23rd, 10:15 a.m.

Though he was in civilian attire when he deplaned at Burlington International, the general expected to be the subject of attention. Vermont's whites represented nearly 96% of the entire population, while blacks and Asians only accounted for a little more than 1% each. So he was not surprised when a couple of children gawked at him, and a teenager made a rude remark. *These children will pay the price for their disrespect soon enough*, he thought.

It wasn't the issue of racism, however, that was of concern, but the two FBI agents he noticed watching him from the terminal building, and others that he didn't see who would be dogging his footsteps. He smiled to himself. *It doesn't matter*, he thought. *By tomorrow, they will no longer be a problem either.*

He and his five staff members were met by a limousine, and driven at well above the speed limit to a luxury resort on the shores of Lake Champlain, about ten miles north of the city. The resort was officially closed for redecorating, but the general was warmly welcomed by the staff. After all, he owned the hotel and resort center. The manager himself met them at the door.

"You cut it very fine, general."

He didn't deign to reply.

By midnight, the entire staff, including hundreds of individuals now in Chinese military uniforms, were safely ensconced in a massive bomb shelter deep beneath the earth, a half-mile uphill from the lake. Every imaginable luxury had been provided, for they planned to remain underground for the next two weeks.

The general's happy company, gathered together to celebrate the approaching events, would especially remember one sentence from his short speech. "We must destroy every remembrance of America's political and religious traditions."

Underworld Caverns

Near Utica, New York
April 23rd, 11:10 a.m.

At Matthew's insistence, Rachel had arranged for the wedding service to take place at noon at Underworld Caverns, about ninety miles west of Albany. She hadn't heard from him in days, and of course her mobile phone wouldn't work beneath nearly two hundred feet of solid rock.

She felt very much alone. Her parents couldn't participate because of illness. Jenna had returned to The Netherlands. And Jaz was in Alaska producing a TV commentary on the rapidly growing Tazlina Glacier, a phenomenon that the global warming advocates had somehow overlooked. As a result, Rachel was only accompanied by a casual acquaintance from college who had somehow heard about the wedding and had, surprisingly, volunteered to serve as her maid of honor.

The ceremony was to be conducted in a colorfully striated rock chamber on the lowest level of the caverns. Ten minutes before they were scheduled to say their vows, Rachel was standing quietly beside the justice of the peace, both of them lost in their own thoughts as they gazed down the cavern at the small boats that plied the underground river.

She was dressed in a simple white cut-away shirt dress, her only jewelry a necklace consisting of a small gold cross hanging from a fine chain. In an effort to remain dry and warm, she had wrapped herself in a clear plastic raincoat. With her dark brown hair combed straight to her waist, and her head crowned with a tiara of fresh daisies, she looked incredibly innocent and vulnerable to her maid of honor as she approached to share her news.

"Rachel," she called, a slight lilt to her voice, "he's not coming!" Then, almost as an afterthought, "I'm sorry."

Rachel looked at her blankly. Then the words sank in and she seemed to go cold.

"Is he all right," she blurted. "He hasn't been in an accident, has he?"

"No," the other woman replied with what she must have supposed was a sympathetic smile. "He called and left a message upstairs. "Oh, Rachel," she gushed, her delight scarcely hidden, "Matt's changed his mind." She waited for some reaction, but receiving none, she offered the coup de grace. "The message says that he's going to marry some senator's daughter this morning."

Rachel stared at her, wanting to imagine that this was some sort of a terrible joke. The other woman, perhaps feeling a bit guilty, repeated lamely, "I'm sorry."

Rachel knew that she was not sorry. As shocked as she was, that much was at least obvious. And Rachel suddenly recalled that this girl had been far more interested in being near Matthew than in associating with her.

The judge felt the tension in the air, and quickly made his excuses. He was obviously unhappy when Rachel told him that her fiance was to have brought a check for his honorarium. After telling her that he'd send a bill, he departed in a huff. She realized that she would probably never see the man again, and for that, at least, she felt absolutely no regret.

Rachel was surprised to discover that she was not suffering any emotional pain. Things suddenly seemed to leap into perspective. It was as though a veil had been lifted and she could put events of the past into perspective. *I'm in shock,* she thought, *but not denial. I don't know why, but I'm not surprised at all.*

Oddly, all she felt was an enormous sense of relief. She realized that she'd been lying to herself, and that she was now suffering the penalty for her self-delusion. At the same time, she felt as though a formerly unrecognized burden had been lifted from her heart.

It was then that Rachel happened to look up at her maid of honor and saw the truth in her eyes. She recalled that the woman was a candidate for a Masters in Psychology, and realized that she was taking more than an abstract interest in this bizarre state of affairs. She could imagine her even now composing a thesis for a college paper: "Naive young woman —caught up in a society for which she is ill-equipped—left waiting at the altar...twenty stories beneath the earth." Rachel realized that her college instructors would probably love it.

She looked again, and it was obvious that the other woman didn't care that her true feelings had been unmasked. Rachel was being examined with a certain detachment, as though she were an insect pinned to a piece of cardboard. The woman obviously didn't care what Rachel thought.

She smiled at Rachel. *She's so innocent that she'd never guess how I'm looking forward to sharing all the details of this debacle with Matt as soon as he returns from his honeymoon. And his very pregnant little wife will never guess that I'm interested in satisfying some of her wifely responsibilities as well.*

What this woman didn't realize was that Rachel was not nearly so naive as she supposed. She had looked carefully into Matthew's background and discovered that, though he was far from a lilly white innocent, she knew that most of his reputation was carefully contrived by those around him.

At that moment, Rachel sensed something of the manipulator in this woman who pretended friendship in order to gain personal advantage, but she refused to give the woman the satisfaction of exposing her feelings. They were alone now, away from the normal flow of tourist traffic, and Rachel's smile suddenly morphed, frightening the petite woman.

"Rachel?" It wasn't a question, nor even a plea for understanding. It was an expression of trepidation.

"You'd better go."

The look she gave Rachel in return was venomous, but there was something of fear in her eyes as well. Without a word, she whirled and made her way up the tunnel, her high heels clattering on the stone floor of the cavern. Rachel's eyes followed her with indifference as the woman pressed the elevator call button, and after several minutes, disappeared from sight.

Rachel wished she had someone with whom she could candidly discuss her situation. She didn't want just anyone to talk with, but someone who would laugh and cry with her, a kindred spirit with whom she could dismantle the relationship, deal with it dispassionately, dissect it, and finally help her discard the pieces. There was undeniably an emotional aspect to this, of course, and it left Rachel with a sense of painful rejection, of both unworthiness, and guilt.

At least she didn't need to suffer for having been soiled, and she was suddenly very glad that she'd never allowed Matthew to have physical relations with her. For while she accepted the fact that she had just been jilted, she also understood that it was not her fault. She was not only older, but much wiser.

The pent-up emotions she was experiencing might have accounted for the rebellion against authority that she exhibited a few minutes later—a reaction that would ultimately save her life. For the moment, however, the desire to avoid anyone she knew resulted in her turning away from the elevator and heading down the walkway toward the underground stream.

Back Bay Museum of Fine Art

Boston, Massachusetts
April 23rd, 11:48 a.m.

Unlike the millions who were immediately and radically impacted, she was lost in her work and totally oblivious of the events occurring above her head.

She was making a list of paintings she would recommend for a special showing for the following month. These were simply her recommendations, but because they were lazy, and they trusted her judgment, the executive committee would probably follow them. And, if anyone complained about the selection, they could always blame it on her.

The vault in which she worked was deep beneath the streets of Boston, designed to protect against any imaginable disaster. Temperature and humidity were carefully controlled to guarantee longevity to the priceless treasures stored there.

It was a new chamber, designed to satisfy insurance carriers and security experts, and was virtually self-contained.

The museum had a large permanent collection, and when collections borrowed from other museums were displayed on the main floor, pieces from upstairs were brought down here for safe keeping.

In the event of a blackout, even electricity would be automatically generated so that the air conditioning, electrostatic filtering system, and the sump pumps used to remove ground water, would never be interrupted. Unfortunately, there was no warning of the unfolding catastrophe, and therefore the staff never had an opportunity to move anything from the museum above down to the vault.

Elizabeth loved the vault. She was isolated eight stories below the museum's main floor. Workers had their own kitchenette to prepare snacks or lunches when they had to work below for extended periods. And now there was a veritable feast awaiting those who were to gather later in the day.

At about ten that morning, the caterer's assistants had dropped off food for a large buffet, leaving all the perishables in ice chests they'd provided. There was to be an open house, a sneak preview of the state papers, for the mayor and other prominent community leaders at 7 p.m. The caterers had begun their deliveries early because they had so many clients scheduled that day, and they were working around the clock. They were to return later to actually cater the meal.

Of course there were no windows, but it seemed airy because it was a large facility with high ceilings. There were three rooms, plus the kitchenette, the elevator and the rest rooms. The main room was about forty by eighty. It was like an art studio with high ceilings and natural lighting so that hues were viewed as accurately as possible. There were paintings hanging on the walls, sculptures setting on the floor and on pedestals, unopened wooden crates, racks of priceless paintings, and stacks of packing materials.

The second and third rooms were each half the size of the main room, with one area used to crate, uncrate, and store valuable works. It had a corner set apart where restoration work could be done when qualified experts were available.

Elizabeth watched as the two federal curators removed the titanium cabinets containing the state papers from the packing crates in which they were shipped. They were very forthcoming, and it was pretty interesting to learn how the technology for storing very old historic documents had advanced.

When she'd visited the British Museum, she'd seen a lot of old-fashioned machines with pens riding back and forth across rolls of graph paper, recording the temperature and humidity in the rooms that contained ancient treasures, such as the Rosetta Stone and Egyptian mummies.

These people from Washington, however, had far more sophisticated gear. They had sensors hooked up to laptops that not only showed the status in the rooms, but second by second, the conditions inside the cabinets that contained the state papers.

Eager to see something of Boston's historic past, the federal agents deserted her to go out and wander Boston's Freedom Trail. As they were leaving, she asked them why they'd left a small tank of argon and a number of large metallic envelopes on a work table.

"We always carry them in case of an emergency."

"I don't understand."

"Well, let's say that one of the cabinets springs a leak.

We'd very carefully remove the document and slip it into the slot in one of those custom-made envelopes."

"Does something like that happen often?"

"Oh, no. We've never had an emergency that demanded their use, but we're required to keep them on hand."

"Well, what would happen if something happened while you are gone?"

"You aren't going to tell anyone we sneaked out, are you?"

"Oh, no. I just wondered."

"Well, the odds of anything going wrong are infinitesimal. And any leak is apt to be extremely slow, so we'd have hours, maybe even days, to take care of it. In most cases, we'd just seal the display cabinet with a special cement."

Then he laughed. "I'll tell you what. If we don't return before one of these springs a leak, here's what you do. Unscrew the back panel, lift out the thin graphite board that the document is attached to, slide it into one of these envelopes, pull the waxed strips off the seals, fold them over, and then tape it up."

The other guy said, "Jack! You shouldn't tell anyone that, not even in joking."

"Who's joking?" He glanced over at me. "You do know I'm joking, right?"

"Of course. I'd be terrified to handle these documents. I know you're kidding."

Then the other fellow piped up. "Since it's all in fun, don't forget to tell her how we'd replace the air in the envelope with argon gas."

And they did.

Then she asked, "Wouldn't the argon leak out?" And Jack answered, "It might. That's why we'd peal this big vinyl circle off the back of the envelope, and press it down over the valve. That would seal the valve and keep the gas in for several months."

And with that, they told her, "Goodbye," and got on the elevator to the surface.

She walked into the third room. It was broken up into four areas—a small office, a kitchenette, a lounge and two bath rooms. These were equipped with showers so that workers could clean up after completing a particularly dirty project.

One of the reasons they were able to borrow great works was because of this incredibly secure facility. There were guards at the top of the stairway and by the elevator doors, around the clock. Only authorized individuals could get near the room.

After the federal employees left, she completed preparations for the presentation, and was just taking it easy. She stood for a long time in front of the titanium cabinets in which America's great state papers were displayed.

She'd asked them, "Have they always been displayed in the National Archives?" Their answer had surprised her.

"Only since the 1950s. The *Declaration of Independence,* for example, has actually been displayed in dozens of other places over the past two centuries, including Baltimore, Washington, and Philadelphia. And in 1777 it even went to Lancaster, Pennsylvania for a day. You get a proper sense of its importance as a national treasure when you learn that it was stored at Fort Knox during World War II.

"How many times has it been to Boston?"

"That's the funny thing. Even though you hosted the "Boston Tea Party," and the "shot heard round the world" was fired in nearby Lexington, the "Declaration" had never been to Boston."

It was almost noon, when the catering staff returned with more food. A half dozen people, accompanied by an armed guard, rolled additional carts loaded with refrigerated containers off the elevator, then rushed off to another job. "We'll be back in plenty of time to set up for your evening program," they promised.

After they left, she stood there trying to read the old text on those documents, for the first time in her life beginning to appreciate their significance. She'd come to realize that, although she had once been a social activist, she didn't want to change America's basic form of government. If there was to be change, she wanted to be certain, beyond any reasonable doubt, that it would improve the nation, not just change things for the sake of change. It seemed to her that too many opportunists and demagogues had been promising too much for too long, and that they had pretty much ruined America by continually pandering to the worst motives.

She wandered around the room, stopping to gaze at a Hirsch portrait that they'd borrowed from another museum. It had been brought downstairs to make room for the borrowed works being set up for "Patriot Week." It was a wonderful piece of work, but not to her taste, and definitely not to the taste of the president, if their carefully collected gossip on that Harvard alumnus was accurate.

Apart from being involved in the heated tariff disputes with the Chinese and the Europeans, plus his continued ambivalence to the never-ending wars in the Middle East, and his justified concerns about the impeachment hearings taking place, it occurred to her that he probably wouldn't make his scheduled political junket to Boston anyway.

She had just started wandering back toward the lounge, thinking she might lie down for a few minutes, when the lights went out. She stood still in the pitch-dark room, and when the emergency lighting came on, she found that she'd been holding her breath. The lights in the room took on a dull glow, and she continued toward the sofa. Then there was a sustained rumbling, and the floor and walls began to shake. The paint flaked off the ceiling and a thin crack appeared in one wall. At first she thought it was an earthquake, and actually had to fight to keep her footing. She caught hold of the edge of the sofa, and both the sofa and she vibrated across the floor. It was heart-stopping, and she allowed herself to drop onto the sofa so that she wouldn't fall over.

She was waiting to see if the regular lighting system would come back on. Finally the stand-by generator kicked in, and the lights came up again. She looked at her watch. It was just two minutes after noon.

Elizabeth knew that they weren't to use the freight elevator in an emergency, but she pushed the call button to see if it was operating. The indicator light didn't come on, and she didn't hear any machinery operating. It was nearly eighty feet to the main floor, and she wasn't about to climb the stairs, so she went back to the lounge to call the security guards upstairs. There was no answer. For a moment she'd imagined that maybe there were thieves in the building, following some elaborate scheme to walk off with millions in paintings, but she realized that thieves couldn't have caused that crack in the wall.

As she looked around the room, she suddenly realized that what she had down there might have greater intrinsic value than all the paintings and sculptures in America. She ran across the room to shut and lock the security doors that would seal off both the elevator and the stairway. Now she was locked in, but if there were any thieves upstairs, they were effectively locked out. If anyone wanted to speak with her, they would have to contact her by intercom.

Having locked herself in, she went back to the lounge and tried calling the police on the outside line. It was dead. She was pretty shaken, but she had done all she could to warn the authorities and to protect that part of the museum in which she was isolated.

She realized that she hadn't eaten since noon, and that she'd better try to get something down while she had the opportunity. So she opened a couple of the cooler chests, made herself a sandwich, and sat down to eat. She later realized that she'd probably eaten one of the last cold cut sandwiches made in America.

Then she laid down on the sofa to await events, and fell asleep.

Medical Center

Deep River Junction, Vermont
April 23rd, 11:55 a.m.

A coffee-stained paper napkin lay on a small table alongside a wedding ring, a wrist watch, and a ballpoint pen. The soiled napkin offered no key to the unconscious patient's identity, but, because it had been in his pocket, it had been saved by the hospital staff as a matter of policy.

It drifted to the floor in the draft created by the swinging door, as a nurse hurried into the room. She stopped short, and knelt to pick up the scrap, bending in a fashion habitual with her, a manner designed unconsciously to draw attention to her ripe figure.

She was about to throw the paper in a waste basket when she realized it had been written upon. Habitually nosy, she examined it in the dim light. It was a hand-written poem. She stared at the paper for a moment, moved closer to the light, then began to mouth the words aloud, trying half-halfheartedly to understand their meaning:

Oh, precious Lord our Savior,
Be with us through this day;
And keep your hand upon us,
Each thing we do and say.
For we are but your children
And need your guiding hand,
To keep us safely moving
Throughout this sin-filled land.

"Oh, my God!" she laughed as she dropped the napkin back on the chair. "Is this for real?" She looked up at the intern who had stood patiently waiting as she stumbled through the lines of the poem.

He stared intently at her, and shrugged his shoulders. "Religious fanatic," he observed flatly.

The intern was only too happy to overlook her lack of intellect in order to focus on attributes which he valued far more. Ordinarily, the attendant wore an air of studied indifference and forced professionalism, but these affectations were less an indicator of his character than were his dissipated good looks and his intense interest in the young nurse who assisted him. Besides, he'd read the poem and didn't care for it either. What was important was that it might offer a clue as to the patient's identity.

Neither was surprised when their conversation was interrupted by the sound of a siren. The growing number of terrorist attacks across America had resulted in various state governments, in opposition to federal government mandates, rejuvenating their civil defense programs, programs which had been shut down decades before.

When the attendant heard the warning, he gave no thought to his patient. Instead he smiled and said, "Everyone will be looking for a corner to hide in for the next twenty minutes. What's say we make ourselves comfortable in the second floor linen closet?"

She giggled, then nodded toward the patient lying unconscious on the X-ray table. "What about him?"

"He'll be okay. No broken bones. No internal injuries. Just a mild concussion. He's been sedated, and he's got an hour on that IV, so he won't wake up for a while."

Though she had little character, and didn't mind violating a rule or two, she did manifest some of the kindness that was supposed to be characteristic of her calling, so in her haste to leave the room, she took time to spread a blanket over the unconscious patient.

Curiosity aroused, she said, "He's kinda cute. Who is he, anyway?"

"He's too old for you, and he's a nobody. If it weren't for the quality of his clothes, we'd have taken him for a derelict. When the ER called to say that they were sending him down, they had him entered as a John Doe."

The nurse gestured at the chair in the corner, then looked at the intern with a glint of suspicion. "Why are his personal possessions here? They should have been inventoried in Emergency and locked in the vault."

"Between the terrorists and air raid drills, Admin is going wild," he replied. "And we're very short-handed. So ER just pushed him in my direction and said, 'Get him X-rayed.'" His eyes followed hers to the table, and the smile left his face. "Don't look at me! This guy didn't have any wallet when he came in here. No wallet, no ID. Thus, John Doe."

The nurse returned to the X-Ray table to study the unconscious man's face in the dim light. "He looks familiar," she mused.

The intern used her comment as an excuse to lean forward and put his arm around her. He spoke brusquely. "He's nobody. Okay?" A smile blossomed on his face, winter becoming summer, and in his most winning way, he reached for her again—"Come on baby, while they're all chasing their make-believe wars, let's go hide in our favorite pile of linen."

She hung back. "If you're holding out on me...."

"Hey, I'm telling you, he didn't have anything on him but that wedding ring, and I wouldn't touch that with a ten-foot pole; it's even engraved."

"Then why'd you take it off him?"

"I had to. They wanted the hand x-rayed. A little lubricant and it slipped right off." He smiled, slipping the ring on and off his own finger before setting it back on the table. She giggled, then glanced once more at the patient. Taking the intern's hand, she nodded her acquiescence. He opened the door, looked both ways, and they ran for the stairs.

The hospital's written rules were strict concerning care of patients, but the young intern was dedicated first to his own interests. Although an accident victim was not to be left laying inert on a table alone, like a piece of cold meat, this patient was going to have to wait. He would wait for many hours.

Underworld Caverns

Utica, New York
April 23nd, 11:56 a.m.

Rachel realized that she was truly alone, and somehow had to deal with the fact that she'd been jilted ten minutes before her wedding ceremony was to begin.

Matthew didn't even have the decency to tell me himself! she thought.

It was at that moment that she heard an alarm bell begin to reverberate through the caverns. It was a signal reserved for potential flood conditions or the unlikely event of a fire.

Oblivious to the noise and activity around her, she continued to the end of the walkway. It skirted the stream upon which a little fleet of flat-bottomed boats carried tourists up and down what was hyped as "The Subterranean River." She had just passed a sign that read "No guests beyond this point" when an attendant returning a boat up the narrow waterway noticed that she was not an employee. He yelled at her to turn back, but she ignored him. Leaning on the railing, she looked down at the narrow stream that had taken eons to carve this tunnel through the limestone.

Characteristically, she squinted her eyes and bit her lower lip. She sighed, then stepped down into an unoccupied boat that had been left tied there. She turned the key that started the electric motor, and began to move the boat downstream. Her boat rubbed the side of a returning boat being steered toward its moorings by another frantic employee. The man did not slow his boat, but did shout at her.

"Hey lady, you can't take that boat." He slowed his boat, and repeated his warning. "Hey, lady; you've gotta get back to the entrance." Then he added the obvious: "There's some kind of emergency." When she still failed to respond, he shouted at the passengers in his boat. "Catch her boat. Don't let her go by."

As one of the men reached for the gunwale of Rachel's boat, she lifted her foot high, offering the man an immodest glimpse that effectively transfixed him. But when he reached for her ankle, she brought her spiked heel down onto the back of his hand, causing him to shriek in pain. Rachel moved to the opposite side of the boat and pushed the lever forward to get maximum speed from the little electric motor, pulling her boat out of reach of her would-be rescuers. As the gap between the boats widened, she gave no further thought to them. The man who'd tried to grab her ankle was nursing his injured hand, screaming curses at her as his boat moved away upstream. The boat tender added his own denunciation, summing up with, "Next time, visit another cavern!"

A multitude of voices were now raised in hysteria. Someone shouted, "Hurry. We're at war! They just announced it over the PA system." Another, "We've got to get upstairs to the lodge."

Rachel was dealing with issues of her own, and was oblivious to their panic as she made her way to the end of the boat run. It was about five hundred feet downstream and around a curve from where she'd boarded the boat, and was terminated by a small man-made dam that impounded just enough water to float the small fleet of boats. Rachel had no intention of going beyond the dam. She had no intentions at all, except to be alone.

Strange, she thought, *I've lost my fiancé, and now we're at war. I wonder whether he'd be at all useful in this situation.* She made a conscious effort to shake him from her thoughts. Her bizarre circumstances helped her succeed. *We're at war,* she mused. *With whom, I wonder? War or no war; I'm glad I'm not stuck down in this cold damp hole in the dark.*

Sometimes life offers more irony than imagination can anticipate, and at that moment life served up one of its pretty surprises. The lights in the tunnel were suddenly extinguished. It took a moment for the afterglow to fade and for the receptors in her eyes to adjust. Then an impenetrable darkness enveloped her, and a mental fog seemed to penetrate her lungs and heart.

Unless a person has already experienced it, it is impossible to imagine the absolute darkness in an unlighted cave eighteen stories beneath the earth's surface. And when Rachel found herself cast into that circumstance without any warning, she was stripped of her remaining defenses.

Gripped with a primeval terror, she forgot the man who had backed out on his commitment to spend the rest of his life with her. She forgot the war. With eyes wide open, her world had narrowed to what she could see inside her own mind. And the absolute absence of light resulted in her suddenly fertile imagination bringing forth a multitude of terrifying images.

"Oh God!" she cried. "What's happening?" She began shouting. "Help, somebody! Please help me!" But apart from the sound of the water falling over the makeshift dam against which the bow of her boat grated, she heard nothing. Her cries were met with total silence. She screamed shrilly, a sustained wail born of an unwavering conviction that she had been abandoned to a living grave, the screams echoing unheard up and down the tunnels.

Tears poured down her cheeks. Wrapping her arms around herself, she rocked back and forth on the boat seat—a vibrant girl, totally in love with life, and now totally out of control. Too much had happened in too short a time, and her reaction could be attributed as much to her tremendous disappointment and sense of betrayal, as to her fear of the darkness.

She started to scream again, but snapped it off after a few seconds, suddenly determined to regain control of her emotions and deal with the situation. Wheeling about, she almost fell over the gunwale in the darkness. The pain to her shin further sobered her, and resulted in her looking down the tunnel over the top of the dam where she saw a glimmer of light in the distance. She stared for a moment, straining to focus, and realized it must be the outfall of the stream. The brochure stated that "The Subterranean River" ran out of the side of the mountain—the place where the cavern ended. The light at the end of the tunnel was enough to calm her, to make her realize there was a way of escape.

Medical Center

Deep River Junction, Vermont
April 23rd, 12:23 p.m.

He lay unmoving on the X-ray table. The IV bag that was connected to his forearm had long since drained itself. Periodically he moaned and moved about on the hard cold surface.

For a brief period, he was drawn back from the vortex of pain into a blissful sleep of non-awareness. Then a myriad of painful sensations ripped his traumatized spirit. His mind reacted by clouding his perceptions. Time passed, and his subconscious continued to seek oblivion.

Yet, he could not remain in a condition of nothingness indefinitely, for his inborn reflexes fought to keep him actively alive—to identify and heal his hurt—even while masking him from the pain. Ironically, as his senses revived, the pain made him want to escape from reality, but this desire for oblivion was countered by the creeping realization that he couldn't sleep if he had to consciously strive to do so.

A nagging abdominal pressure brought increasing discomfort, but his mind was detached and would not yet permit him to identify a specific need—only general sensations. His body was becoming a world of aches, of stretchings and tearings, and of intermittent searing pain.

Had there been professional help nearby, they might have sedated him, but he was alone with his pain. It was simply there, washing over him like waves sweeping the shore, unremitting, inexorable, and unreasoning. Between the foaming crests he found himself caught in hollows of nirvana. It was when was swept from these hollows onto the crests that his growing consciousness sought to escape—clawing, choking, and thrashing—doing himself more harm than good.

Pain awoke him to more pain. He was in a hurricane of torment, and at its center was a terrible malignant crimson eye that seemed to search his soul, seeking the point of greatest susceptibility, diabolically contriving to torture him in some unmentionable manner. The eye centered itself before his imagination, then spread to the horizons of his apprehension.

His thrashing about simply produced more pain. His endeavors to escape sucked him more deeply into the vortex of agony, but this very pain also began to serve the purpose for which his Creator had established it—to awaken his mind to the needs of his flesh. He became captive to his passion for escape. He sought to evade the terrible screaming vortex of pain that centered itself before the eye of his mind, but by now its wispy ethereal tendrils were becoming grasping, sucking tentacles, creeping downward and within, bringing into existence additional sources of suffering and uncharted territories of torture.

It was hideous. He was being born into a world of pain, a place from which his malaise could not protect him, and where active resistance produced additional torment. Suddenly he saw the image of his children being carried to the ambulances, and he screamed. The image vanished.

He slowly became aware that he was a living being, no longer blessedly disembodied. He had a torso, and limbs, and a head. And that body was wracked with pain. He began to identify the injured areas by the sensations they seemed to produce and radiate. When he sought to shift some part of his body to relieve the suffering, a new agony was discovered in another.

And when the stubborn heroism of consciousness overcame the craven desire for passivity, helpless shame was born. The pressure that had been building for hours was finally released, and for the first time since he was a small child his cheeks burned with the tears of frustration and shame because he had lost control of himself.

Through cracked and swollen lips he croaked a petition

for relief, but his plea for help was met with silence. Blood-encrusted eyelids resisted movement. Newly discovered fingers scrabbled futilely against the cold, smooth surface which formed his bed. A persistent ache behind his right ear was eclipsed by a burning pain in his left arm as he sought to shift his position. He dragged his hand over his chest and discovered a serpentine tangle of flexible tubing taped to his forearm.

Cognitive abilities were returning, and with them a will to awaken and live. Gently he brushed his eyes and felt a thin crust of blood. Carefully tracing a path across his forehead, he discovered a large gauze bandage. He rubbed his eyes again, and discovered that he could open them slightly. Now his senses were offended by the bright light which intermittently invaded them. He turned his head to the side and tried to focus on the offending glare. It seemed to pierce the retinas, to sear his brain. Slowly his eyes adjusted, and he again attempted to survey his situation. Obviously a concussion, he concluded. Can't be too bad if I can reason it out.

He realized that he was in a dimly-lit box of a room, sparsely furnished, deeply shadowed, with yellow walls. A small fixture on a side wall supplied the one source of light. There were two doors, on adjacent walls, and what appeared to be an observation window next to one of them. His eyes grew tired, and he fell back into a fitful sleep.

When he next awoke, he discovered that he was lying on a large table with a complicated system of pipes and cables above his head, and a device which he recognized as an X-ray camera. There was no evidence of anyone else's presence, and he grew angry when he realized that though he appeared to be in a hospital, the personnel were neglecting him. He tried to raise his head to shout, but fell back hard, suffering a blinding flash of pain and a resumption of blessed unconsciousness.

Some time later he relived much of the same awful experience of reawakening, but with far less suffering. Raising his head a second time, he was able to see the source of pain to his left forearm. A clear plastic tube was taped to his wrist and ran to an empty plastic bag hanging from a metal rack.

A needle at the end of the tube was taped where it entered his vein. He began to pick at the adhesive tape with his other hand, fumbling to pull it loose, but the intravenous needle stuck to the tape, and in his groping he yanked it nearly sideways from his arm, causing him to gasp with the pain and pulling him wholly back into the real world. He swallowed the acrid stench of his own bile, as he drew the needle from his arm and let the weight of the tubing drag it flopping to the floor. Then he fainted.

Underworld Caverns

Utica, New York
April 23rd, 12:12 p.m.

Rachel sat rigidly on one of the wooden seats, staring wide-eyed into the darkness, as the boat rocked gently in the current. As her breathing calmed and she was able to reflect on her situation, it occurred to her to begin searching for anything that might help her survive, though she didn't expect to find any emergency equipment stored in the boats. This was, after all, a daytime tourist attraction. She nevertheless rooted around in the bow, and located a tool box that contained a few useful items. The most valuable was a flashlight. It's amazing," she laughed aloud, "what light does to restore one's sanity." With the light in hand, she also discovered a first-aid kit and a candy bar.

She remembered reading that the tunnel continued for some distance below the dam, and that it exited the mountain inside a quarry. Yet as much as she hated the darkness, she was far more frightened of going outdoors and potentially exposing herself to radiation poisoning.

While Rachel slowly chewed the chocolate bar, she closed her eyes, trying to bring to mind pleasant memories. Then she put the boat's transmission in reverse, and ran it slowly back up the stream. Climbing up to the landing, she used the flashlight to make her way back through the cavern to the two elevators. They had been shut down, so she started up the stairway. When she reached the first landing, she found a door bearing a 1960's Civil Defense symbol, and realized that it had once been equipped as a fallout shelter.

Inside, she was surprised to find stacks of survival supplies. Among them she found a radio and a carton of "D" cells. She changed the batteries, but when she turned it on, all she was able to raise was static. Then she noticed a wire hanging from the back of the radio with an alligator clip attached. She clipped it to a water pipe in the corner of the room, spun the tuning dial, and immediately picked up the emergency broadcast network.

The news was not good. According to the report, nuclear weapons had been detonated over several cities, foreign troops were already marching on U.S. soil, and terrorist acts and civil unrest had made the situation even more chaotic.

It was clear to her that she was on her own. She snapped off the radio and tried to comprehend the enormity of the crisis. Then she realized that she needed to put things in proper perspective, to scale them down to her little world, in order to assess her chances of survival.

She realized that if there was radioactive fallout in the area, she was far safer where she was, well below the earth's surface. *What's more,* she decided, *I'm much safer here alone, especially if any of these rations are safe to eat.* And she reasoned, *The first thing I ought to do is inventory anything useful in this room.*

She found a stack of cartons containing folding cots and blankets. They were all shrink-wrapped in plastic, and when she opened one, she was amazed to discover that it was not mildewed. Taking fresh batteries from the carton she'd found earlier, she replaced the ones in her flashlight. Then she opened some cartons of MREs, and found that they were dated less than two years earlier. It occurred to her that the owners of the cavern might well have stashed them here in case of emergency, but if so she couldn't understand why they hadn't come down here to shelter.

Finally, she made up a bed, locked the door, and lay down to sleep. As she lay there, she thought of family and friends, but that almost drove her into a state of despair, so she determined to avoid such thoughts. Then she spent time in prayer. After a while, she fell asleep.

When she awoke, she checked her watch and discovered that she had lost track of time. She no longer knew whether it was 2:27 in the afternoon or 2:27 in the middle of the night. In this world of perpetual darkness, time ceased to exist. She decided to spend as much time in sleep as possible.

At one point she realized that she must have been awake nearly forty hours. At another, she thought she slept over twenty-four hours straight. It was evidently a phenomenon of living in total darkness. She began to keep a calendar, slashing off time in twelve-hour cycles. It's odd, she mused, how time seems to pass much faster down here.

There was enough food to feed a large number of people, though the flavor was poor. When she grew weary of the MREs, she tried canned goods. The tops were not swollen, so she didn't fear ptomaine poisoning. Amongst the cartons of food, she found a case of flashlights which she used sparingly because the batteries were old.

She'd taken it for granted that, if the bottled water ran out, she'd be able to use water from the underground river. The second or third day, she heard water flowing, and opened the door to discover that the caverns below her had flooded, and the water had risen so much that the surface was only three steps below her landing. The flooding lasted only a couple of days, and it never reached the level of the shelter, but to play it safe she carried a cot up to the next landing and slept there until the water receded.

Although she wasn't worried about drowning, the possibility occurred to her that the flood water might contain nuclear fallout. She found a radiation detector among the supplies in the shelter, and after she'd read the instructions and inserted new batteries, she discovered that the levels were negligible.

Back Bay Museum of Fine Art

Boston, Massachusetts
April 23rd, 12:22 p.m.

Unable to sleep, Elizabeth lay on the sofa for about ten minutes, wondering why there weren't people swarming all over the place?

She tried the phone again. There was no dial tone. She didn't bother with her cell phone because she was beneath a massive barrier of concrete, steel, and earth. She went over to the elevator and pushed the call button. Still nothing. She again tried the intercom. No response there either, even though she knew that at least two armed officers from the Department of Interior were to be on guard at all times. It didn't make sense, and she was really growing concerned.

Although the museum storage and work areas were more than eighty feet beneath the streets of Boston, there were ordinarily good communications from the surface, including telephone, cable TV, and a radio with an antenna that reached the roof of the museum. The TV was out, so she tried the radio. The Boston stations were not broadcasting, but she twisted the dial until she located a station in Portland, Maine. An announcer was warning viewers to get underground—to protect themselves from the first wave of radioactive dust.

She was stunned. What was happening? Another Chernobyl? The Third World War? She found a notebook and pen, and began writing down the announcer's recommendations. He was now speaking very rapidly. She'd recorded a half-dozen recommendations when he stopped to say that he'd just learned that another attack was imminent. As he began his next sentence, the signal was lost.

Elizabeth sat staring at the radio, the irritating noise it

made lost in the white noise of her own confusion. In an attempt to locate other stations still on the air, she pressed the search button, but it was fruitless. She didn't know how long it was before she came to herself, probably just a couple of minutes. She turned off the set and attempted to assess her situation.

She picked up the list she'd made.

- Prepare for at least two weeks in isolation.
- Locate an underground shelter with at a foot or more of earth or concrete surrounding you. *Well, I've got that!*
- Store at least one gallon of water per day per person for drinking and cooking (washing extra).
- Gather at least a two-week supply per person. (Salt makes you thirsty.)
- Remember blankets, flashlights and batteries, and a portable radio.

She looked around. A quick inventory revealed that the caterer had stacked cases of bottled water, soft drinks, wine, fruit juices, and beer in ice-filled chests for the reception. There were even several cases of liquor. Elizabeth didn't care for alcohol, but would have skipped it anyway because it would both dehydrate her and take the edge off her thinking. It might be useful in an emergency to disinfect wounds, but she reasoned that the bottled water and fruit juices would meet her needs.

The first action she took was to remove anything from the kitchen's two-door refrigerator that she considered empty calories, and replaced them with the most nutritive foods the caterer had left in the ice chests. She was confident that the refrigerator would operate until the stand-by generator ran out of fuel. *Whenever that might be,* she thought ruefully.

Then she went to the door marked, "No Admittance, Mechanical Room," and turned off the electricity to the water heater. Shutting off the inlet and outlet valves would keep it from draining, she thought, and she could access that precious water by opening the drain valve at the bottom. She proved her theory by filling a pot she found in the kitchen. When she tried the faucets on the sink, the municipal water was still running, so she filled several of the now-empty cooler chests with water. A couple of drops of disinfectant in each would prevent bacteria from growing. She would use this water to give herself sponge baths each day.

Elizabeth figured it would grow pretty chilly once the heat went off, so she gathered the coats and other odd clothing people had left laying about, as well as a blanket she found folded in a cabinet. This would have to do for bedding. Then she settled down to remain underground for the next two weeks. She couldn't stop imagining what was happening above her head. Although she'd often been forced by circumstances to keep to herself, the idea of being isolated for two weeks, and perhaps never seeing another living human being, was disheartening. Things didn't work out in quite that way.

Medical Center

Deep River Junction, Vermont
April 23rd, 2:52 p.m.

When he next awoke he felt somewhat better. He rolled over onto his side and half-slid, half-fell from the X-ray table to the floor. Kneeling there, he leaned his elbows on the table, head in hands, and was swept with nausea. It seemed obvious that he'd suffered a concussion.

After several minutes, he reached for the clipboard which hung from the end of the X-ray table. His eyes refused to remain in focus, and he was suddenly violently ill, throwing up on the side of the table. Then he slid to the floor, moaning with the pain from his head injury. He began to shiver, and realized he had to get warm. Pulling himself back into a kneeling position, he reached for a folded blanket that lay on one end of the table. It took him a moment to wrap it around himself, and was pleased to discover that his eyes were focusing better.

Once again, he noticed the clip board hanging from the apparatus at the end of the table. Tipping the board toward the light, he futilely searched the page for a clue as to the extent of his injuries, struggling to interpret the notations concerning blood pressure, pulse, and temperature.

The attending physician's scrawl was better than most. He had written, "Possible skull fracture. Concussion, left cerebral hemisphere; X-ray." Reading down the chart, he understood that he had been treated for shock. His injuries, except for the swelling on his head, were described as minor.

His eyes moved to the top of the page, and he was struck forcibly by what was written beside *Patient's name*—"John Doe."

"All they had to do was look in my wallet," and his hand slipped across the hospital gown to where the inside coat pocket of his suit would have been. He laughed derisively at his own helpless disorientation. *It must be around here someplace,* he thought, *but it doesn't really matter. Now that I'm awake, they won't need my ID. I can tell them myself, and they can phone my—phone my....*

He grasped the table, squeezing the stainless steel support as though to force from it a name, a face, any memory. His eyes returned to the clipboard, now impossible to focus on because of the shaking of his hand.

"That's it," he said aloud with conviction. The movement of his jaw increased his headache. He thought, "I've suffered a momentary lapse of memory because I've banged my head. I'm in shock, that's all. I'll be Okay. I'll remember my name in a little while. And once I have my own name, other facts will come back to me."

Then the awful realization of his amnesia caught him, and he transitioned from concern to fear. He slid the clipboard part way onto the table, but it fell to the floor. *This too will pass,* he assured himself. *I'll be all right. I just have to be calm. I just need to accept it, and not worry about it, and I'll be okay*

His eyes returned to the clipboard. Picking it up, he realized that his hands were a bit steadier. He pulled it close, focusing on other handwriting, more precise than that of the doctor. Someone, probably a nurse, had filled in data dealing with his vital statistics: Sex—Male; Age—approximately 35-40; Height—5'-10"; Weight—155 lbs; Eyes—brown; Hair—brown; Distinguishing marks—Surgical scar, lower right abdomen.

He ran his hands over his body, even parting the hospital robe to examine the abdominal scar, looking at himself in wonder, trying to become reacquainted. It was like seeing himself for the first time. A feeling of unreality swept over him, as though a stranger had invaded his body, or he were a stranger in someone else's skin. His eyes remained over one phrase for some time: "Cause of Injury(s)—Automobile

Accident." There was no description of the car, the location, the incident, or of anyone else who might have been involved.

He could see, but he was blind to reality. He was beginning to comprehend the present, but he could not imagine the past. He knew that he existed, but did not know who he was. He did not even know where he was. Well, there it was, at the top of the page, *The Community Hospital, Deep River Junction, Vermont.*

Cold and hunger took control of his decision-making processes, and his anger fanned the fires of his recuperation. He was angry at the physicians and nurses who would leave a patient alone like this—perhaps to die.

A few moments passed, and he heard a distant rumble, as though a severe thunderstorm were rolling across the mountains. The lights blinked, then went out. Not only have they forgotten that I'm here, he thought, but some idiot had turned out the lights. His response was to shout in anger, but it was little more than a croak. He knelt down, a prisoner of ignorance, not knowing what lay beyond the X-ray room door. He was immersed in a black void, surrounded by the demons of his own imagination. He realized that he had heard another of those thunder rolls earlier, even through his semi-conscious state, and it had vibrated the table upon which he lay. Only it wasn't so much like thunder, but like an enormous prolonged explosion heard from far away.

Now he heard a different sound, still like thunder, but closer and far less severe. The muted sound of machinery somewhere nearby rumbled, then settled into a steady throbbing. A light began to glow on the wall near the door, then came to full brightness. The sudden unaccustomed glare seemed to pierce his eyes like a knife point going to his brain, and for a moment the pain swept all thought away. He knelt by the edge of the X-ray table, eyes closed, head in hands, rocking back and forth, moaning in distress.

Back Bay Museum of Fine Art

Boston, Massachusetts
April 24th, 7:22 a.m.

Elizabeth had just stretched out on the sofa for another nap when there was a horrific banging on the security doors that sealed off the stairway to the surface. She didn't respond, frightened that it might be someone intent on stealing artwork.

Then she heard a muffled voice. "Elizabeth, are you there?" More pounding. "Elizabeth, it's me, Dan Benton. Open up."

Benton was another curator, a conservator. He was actually extremely gifted, for he not only cleaned and repaired paintings for the museum, but he had made some amazingly accurate copies of masterpieces. She had mixed feelings about letting him in because he had a bad reputation among the other employees, but she knew that she couldn't leave him out there to starve. It was only fair to share her food and water with him. Her decision turned out to be a terrible mistake. When she opened that emergency door, her own personal terror began.

The moment he came through the door, he laughingly shouted, "All the world's going to hell!" And then he hollered, "Let's party!" When she looked at him in disbelief, he said, "Eat, drink, and be merry, for tomorrow we die." And with that, he raised a whiskey bottle to his lips.

He was filthy, covered with dust, his normally crisp white shirt soiled and torn, his tie loose. His thinning hair was mussed, his dirty face scratched and stained by drying blood. All that, along with his sunken chest and pot belly, presented a truly pathetic countenance. In spite of that, he was still a very big, very imposing man, and any woman might have been frightened to be alone with him at any time, much less under these circumstances.

She'd always avoided having anything to do with him because she considered him a very nasty number, and his drunken behavior at that moment did nothing to alter her opinion. Her response was measured and cold. "I have no intention of eating or drinking, much less being merry, while thousands, maybe even millions of people are dying out there." And, in measured tone she added, "And I certainly have no intention of dying if I can avoid it."

"Hey, sure, relax. I was only kidding."

"It didn't sound like kidding," she answered evenly.

"Look, we're in this together, whether we like it or not," he replied, an edge to his voice. Let's try to get along, okay?"

"Get along?"

"We're here together," and he waved his arms wide, the liquor splashing to the floor from the carelessly held bottle. "So you don't have to worry anymore, because big old Dan Benton is gonna take care of you, baby. And I do mean, he's gonna take care of you."

"I don't think so," she responded, trying to hide her fear. "I want you to take some of this food and water, and then get out of here and leave me alone."

"Oh, not a chance, sweetheart. We're in this together now." It seemed to her that he was leering at her as he said, "I have no intention of going anywhere."

She glared at him, angry at herself for unlocking the door and letting him in, beginning to realize just how dangerous he might be. He had the reputation of being an unprincipled man, divorced, with three children who were continually in and out of trouble, and it was said that he'd been able to keep his job at the museum only by holding something over the head of one of the directors. She had found it a struggle to keep their relationship on a professional level. And she had always tried to keep a table or chair between them when in the same room because he was notorious for his wandering hands.

Elizabeth tried to change the subject by asking him what was going on upstairs, but he ignored her question.

"Hey, how about a drink?" he asked. "It'll help you loosen up, forget all these problems."

"No," she responded. "I don't want a drink, and I don't want to forget my problems. I want to understand them. Just tell me what happened up in the museum."

"You always were a prissy uptight female."

"I beg your pardon?"

"I know all about you," he sneered. "Why everyone here knew all about you." He dropped onto the sofa, suggestively patting the cushion next to him.

"What do you mean, you know all about me," she demanded.

"You're a rich little witch from an old New England family whose ancestors traveled to the new world on the Mayflower. Your people were Boston Brahmins and Beacon Hill—old money, old culture, and definitely old contempt for your fellow workers, all born below your station."

"That's not true!"

Drunk as he was, he could sense that he was getting under her skin. “You mean, you're not rich? Or you're not a witch?”

And she bit, making an effort to defend herself.

“I'm not like my family.” And her voice trailed off for a moment.

“Sure. I'll write that down.”

“Yes, you do that.” She was thinking back to the time when she broke with her family, but she wasn't go to give him the satisfaction of sharing that information.

She had, from the time she'd been a teenager, been undergoing a change in attitude. Like most teenagers, she wanted to earn her independence, but she had also hoped for her family's approval and occasional expressions of love. Unfortunately the combination of their self-centered life-style, controlling natures, and incredible stinginess drove her further and further from her parents. She finally rebelled against the strictures placed upon her by a family intent only upon its wealth, political power, and position in the blue book.

She resolved to make a name for herself on her own. It was difficult, not because she lacked the talent or determination, but because people who recognized her continually sought to reap whatever advantage they could from her family by helping to open doors for her.

The last straw came one morning when she found her father on his private balcony with a cup of coffee and copies of “The Boston Herald” and The Wall Street Journal.” She knew that he expected others to leave him alone during this sacred rite. For a full two minutes, he left her standing there while he completed the reading of an article, then stared at her coolly as he drained his coffee cup.

“What is so important that you interrupt me now? he finally demanded, his eyebrows drawing together in a manner that always brought uncertainty and even fear to the hearts of his subordinates.

She stood erect, taking visible control of herself. “I've come to tell you that I will not be attending mother's school,” she replied.

He slammed his cup down on the table, breaking the handle, and causing his spoon to skip across the cloth napkin. His voice almost seethed with menace as he replied quietly to his rebellious daughter, “You most certainly will!”

“No, I won't,” she replied, her stubborn resolve not quite overcoming the slight quaver in her voice.

“You've always been a willful daughter, but you will do as I say for your own good.”

“That's not true,” she shot back, all uncertainty gone. “I've always been a good daughter, submitting to you whether you were right or wrong—and rarely for my own good—but not this time.”

He stared at her for a moment, but she did not flinch nor turn away, so he undertook his time-tested method of winning by intimidation.

“You will go wherever we decide to send you, or suffer severe consequences.”

“Then I'll suffer the severe consequences,” was all she had answered, and turned to walk out of his life.

She had anticipated his response, and already had a bag packed and stashed in the coat closet by the front door, and her not insubstantial and secret savings in a money belt fastened securely beneath her skirt. A taxi was waiting at the curb, and drove her to the station. She left her sports car behind, knowing that she could no longer afford insurance and registration, much less gasoline and maintenance. Besides, she realized, it would only make it easier for her father's private investigators to locate her.

She caught a train to the little college town where she had awarded a full academic scholarship. She had shown remarkable promise as an artist, so when she chose a school with a respected art program, she gained ready acceptance.

She'd managed to divulge as little information about herself as possible, and it had not been immediately recognized that she was the daughter of John Ross. It seemed important to her that she could win admission on her own merits, though she realized that it wouldn't be long before her parents discovered her whereabout. *They hate to be defied, and will do almost anything to get even with me,* she realized, but she doubted that they would pressure the school to throw her out. *It wouldn't look good in the media,* she thought, but she knew what was at stake.

She had been right. Once her parents had learned of her enrollment in a school with an excellent reputation, they took no overt action. Besides, they were saving more money than most people made in a lifetime by her not attending her mother's Ivy League school. They did, however, gain influence with the administration of the college she was attending by making an anonymous contribution for a new art center. As a result, the administration kept them aware of Elizabeth's progress. They went so far as having someone on staff continually monitor her activities, both academic and personal, without her knowledge.

In spite of this, Elizabeth fought blithely on, unaware of the pressures being brought both for and against her. Her many accomplishments seemed the more impressive because her families' vast wealth disqualified her from securing additional assistance.

Elizabeth was able to complete the program by exhausting her secret cash reserves, taking out student loans, and working part-time. And she somehow still earned academic honors. She did not contact her parents during those four difficult years, and they failed to recognize the growing core of bitterness she had toward them. Nor did they comprehend the strength of character that resulted through her perseverance and pain.

As time passed, her rebellion had unexpected consequences. She rubbed elbows with, and gained sympathy for, the so-called working class. Along the way she learned the value of a dollar, and actually came to hold the idle rich—and particularly her own family—in contempt. Nonetheless, during her first two years of college, the overweening pride and self-righteousness that had been inculcated in her from childhood often caused her to mock and haze the less fortunate.

When she completed the four-year program, graduating cum laude, she had a choice of several jobs that had high visibility. She was offered a position as a writer and photographer for a major art monthly and another as a sales rep for a respected auction company. She rejected both because she discovered that they wanted to capitalize on her family's name rather than on her knowledge and ability.

So she instead secured the position in the struggling Back Bay Art Museum as an assistant curator. It was only later that she learned that her parents were still meddling in her life, not because they cared for her, but because they would be embarrassed if she took a position that didn't have a minimum of prestige and dignity. So in order to smooth her path, they were secretly making substantial endowments to the museum.

"Yes, of course," the assistant director nodded to signal agreement with what she secretly considered the fantastic idealism of this gullible child.

There isn't the least chance that we'd purposely offend you, you beautiful but naïve young thing. The largesse coming to this museum as a result of your parent's secret patronage guarantees you this job.

As far as the director was concerned, there was no hypocrisy involved. This was a simple matter of quid pro quo. You scratch my back, and I'll scratch yours! Everyone knew it took the patronage of wealthy people to maintain an art museum. So the management had agreed with Elizabeth's parents to help protect the simple child from own naivete.

Dan Benton knew these facts. Elizabeth did not. So when he mocked her for riding on her father's coat tail to get her job, she was enraged.

"Why you dunderhead, I earned this job, and I've proven it!"

He was delighted to discover that he'd made her lose her self-control. She had a reputation for being unflappable.

"Why do you think Benoit backed off from chasing you? He demanded.

This shocked her even more. She didn't realize that anyone was aware that Ms.Benoit had attempted to seduce her. She believed that what kept that particular director from pursuing her was her own masterful handling of a potentially messy situation, and she said as much.

"Not at all!" Benton corrected her. "She wasn't afraid of you. She was afraid of losing her job because, if you complained, your family would cease its financial support."

"What financial support?"

"Oh, come now. Do you mean to tell me that you don't know your parents have been giving large sums to the museum in return for your having a cushy job here."

"I know no such thing," she shouted in retort.

"Well, get used to it, because that's exactly the way it was."

Elizabeth was struck dumb. She remembered how her relationship with Benoit had reached an uncomfortable point where Elizabeth had communicated with her as little as possible, only in monosyllables, and then only in direct response to questions about the work at hand. This had gone on for a period of about two weeks.

Elizabeth expected to be discharged because Benoit had a lot of influence with the museum, but during a conversation with a young intern, she learned that there was no way she was going to get herself fired "...because your dear old dad and mum are almost single-handedly supporting the museum." Elizabeth angrily disputed the claim, treating it as an insult. When she'd had time to cool down, she realized that it was very likely true.

To test the hypothesis, she'd said some very nasty things to Benoit when she contrived to run into her in the lady's powder room. Instead of getting angry, or firing Elizabeth, the woman attempted to placate her. When Elizabeth persisted, and poured insult on insult, Benoit began to cry.

"Please," she pleaded, "I need this job. Please don't share your feelings about me with anyone else." And then, to Elizabeth's amazement and shame, the woman told her, "I'll do anything you ask. I won't assign you any work you don't want to do." Then, with tears in her eyes, she fled the room.

The head curator, realizing that something was amiss

between the two, decided that he needed Elizabeth's financial connections far more than the assistant director's professional skills, so he planned to let Benoit go. When Elizabeth overheard of his plan to terminate the woman, she found herself coming to her aid.

"I really wish you wouldn't let her go," she said. "Ms. Benoit is very good at what she does, and her dismissal would be a loss to the museum." The curator was both surprised and relieved to hear this, for he didn't want to have to try to add the woman's responsibilities to his own.

At first, he wondered whether he'd misjudged Elizabeth, and that she and the assistant director were both of the same persuasion. Then he realized that Elizabeth was a nicer person than he'd suspected, and she simply had the best interests of the museum and, yes, the assistant director, at heart. For a few days, he too had fantasized about having a relationship with her, but it became very clear that such a possibility was fraught with risks and out of the question.

Elizabeth actually had little interest in any personal relationships of any kind. It was her ambition to prove herself and move on to another museum where she'd be hired for her skills, not for her name. So she was continually reading and studying. She even gave some thought to changing her name. When she could, she traveled to other museums at her own expense. She was able to work out arrangements for short-term trades of major works between her museum and those in other cities. Her detachment, her cold professionalism, and her integrity soon earned her the title, "Elizabeth Ice."

And now Dan Benton was mocking her. She let her eyes rove around the room, looking anywhere but at him. She found herself focusing on the new crack in the wall where ground water had begun seeping in. *Why am I carrying on so,* she wondered. *It's all over! We're at war, my family is very likely dead, and the museum will probably never reopen. Benton's insults mean nothing.*

Her thoughts returned to her true worth. She'd added value to the museum. Her greatest coup was arranging to bring the original autographs of the Declaration of Independence and the Constitution to the city, an achievement that her employers recognized as unequaled in the museum's history. As it turned out, the documents would never be exposed to the people of Boston. The last person to look upon them would be Elizabeth Ross.

Medical Center

Deep River Junction, Vermont
April 24th, 7:24 a.m.

After some time, he again became conscious of his surroundings. He dragged himself to his feet, then staggered across the room toward a small table. Leaning stiff-armed against its surface, he fought back the bile that rose in his throat. He struggled to focus on the objects laying there, hoping that they would offer a clue to his identity.

There was a ball-point pen, a wedding ring and a paper napkin. The napkin had words scribbled upon it, but it held no key to his identity. It looked like a poem. Words had been scratched out and changed. He was not sure he wanted to read it, but felt it might offer a clue.

He stared at the napkin. It was a poem, and sounded like words from an old hymn. Then he realized again that he'd probably written the words, and whether it was something from memory, or something he had composed, it had probably seemed important to the man he'd been.

On impulse, he took the pen and copied the last line of the poem. He could not really compare the similarities in the writing closely because of the tears in his eyes, but there was no doubt that the writing was his. An unfathomable anguish testified to his authorship.

He returned the note to the table, and with shaking hands lifted the ring that lay beside it. It offered little to satisfy his growing hunger to know himself. It was simply a gold band. He held it under the magnifying glass of the examination light so that he could read the letters engraved on the inside surface—"CC & DR, and a date." That was all. Just the initials, and, presumably, the year of the wedding.

Should he assume his initials were listed first, because he was the husband, or hers, because she was the woman? He stared at them, expecting some sort of image to arise in his mind. "DR or CC?" He tried to concentrate on the DR, to envisage a woman's face or body. Nothing. What's more, his mind seemed to stray to other things, as though it was avoiding the memory. He determined to take care of first things first, permitting his mind to settle its own debates as it was able. Yet he couldn't help wondering what names the initials might represent.

He pulled himself to his feet, and staggered to the door. After hanging on to the casing for a moment, he left the X-ray room to make his way slowly down the hall. He moved on, sliding his hand along the chair rail to maintain his balance. Exit signs and night lights were operative wherever he turned, but the standard lighting was out. He concluded that the standby generator only supported night lights and, perhaps, operating room and emergency equipment.

He didn't find anyone, and he drew a line at entering a door labeled "Morgue." When he came to the elevators, he discovered that he was on the basement floor. The elevators, of course, were not operating, and, as weak and dizzy as he was, he decided not to try the stairs. For a fleeting moment he wondered if the Christian rapture might had occurred. He laughed hollowly at the prospect, thinking what an eerie and unprecedented thing it is to discover oneself virtually alone in a hospital.

As he pushed through a double set of doors, the odor of hot food seized him with such impact that his long-neglected hunger overwhelmed him. He walked quickly toward the vacant serving line, stepped around the end of the steam table, lifted a lid, and grabbed a warm leg from a tray of fried chicken. He was salivating even before he bit into the succulent meat, and was struck by the thought that nothing had ever tasted more delicious.

Chewing hungrily, he became aware of a muttering sound in the food preparation area. He let out a sigh of relief as he realized that there was someone else in the building. Righteous indignation fought with joyous relief as he pushed open the kitchen door. He opened his mouth to greet the occupants, but his words echoed emptily from the shining ceramic walls.

The room was unoccupied. The voice he'd heard was coming from a radio that sat on a stainless steel shelf. Where was the staff that should have been preparing meals for the patients? He moved closer, and caught the speaker's voice in mid-sentence.

"...unable to advise you of the extent of the attack, or the losses sustained....massive evacuations to safe areas, according to long– standing Executive Orders....last report from

Washington advised that the President may not have made it to Air Force One."

He stood in the midst of a huge institutional kitchen, pans of food in the steam table, a half-eaten chicken leg in one hand, his hospital robe hanging open, and listened to a newscaster telling him that the nation was in the midst of a war. He simply couldn't take it in. When he forced his mind back to the radio, the commentator was advising people to secure canned foods, medical supplies, blankets, sanitary items, and, especially, water.

"Stay under cover for at least two weeks and...." The message was interrupted by a short burst of static, then there was just the hum of a poorly tuned radio.

He stood there in stunned comprehension. This, he thought, made the trauma of 911 seem like a routine fender bender. He wondered how many Christians might be standing around idle, waiting for Jesus to appear in the clouds and rapture them to heaven. Then he wondered why he wondered that. Was he a Christian? He thought so, but how would he know that? He shook his head in an attempt to clear the cobwebs, and the pain that resulted from the movement almost brought him to his knees and reminded him that he'd suffered a head injury.

His mind returned inexplicably to the thought that many Christians would be disillusioned if the United States were destroyed in a world war, rather than their being transported to heaven in the rapture. So many of them mistakenly considered America the center of the Christian world, the apple of God's eye, and lived in great comfort while many of the world's Christians had been struggling for years to survive in the midst of famine and war. *Why had we felt that way?* he wondered. He found himself echoing the words of Christ: "You err, because you do not know the Scriptures."

The United States, he realized, *once figured largely in God's plan because it helped protect and preserve the Apple of His eye, the Jews in Israel, and because it helped sustain world peace. Beyond that, Americans invested a lot of money in promoting world missions and doing good works on behalf of the less privileged, but that had all begun to change in the recent past. If these are indeed the end times described in the Bible,* he thought, *then the United States has ceased taking a meaningful role.* And, he realized with some shame, *we have failed dismally.*

The attitude of the people might well be described with the words, "in the latter days, men will be lovers of themselves," and "the love of many shall wax cold." Christians had become mocked by a majority of citizens, crime was rampant, unborn babies had been murdered by the millions, a preoccupation with perverse sex had destroyed marriages and families, and even trickled down into the classroom where teachers corrupted young students. The perversion certainly exceeded that of Sodom and Gomorrah.

God has patiently withheld his judgment, he thought, *but is finally allowing America to stew in its own juices. Well,* he thought uncharitably, *a lot of people might be going to heaven today, but not, as a result of the rapture.*

"Then what is this?" a voice seemed to ask.

He stood stock still for a moment, looking vainly for the person who'd asked the question, and found himself replying aloud to the empty room.

"Perhaps these are the events that will immediately precede the end, the times that Jesus warned of when he said 'You will be hearing of wars and rumors of wars. See that you are not frightened, for those things must take place, but that is not yet the end.'"

Then, realizing that millions of people might be dying this very day, he quoted Christ's sobering words from his Sermon on the Mount: "He causes His sun to rise on the evil and the good, and sends rain on the righteous and the unrighteous."

If his feverish maunderings were correct, then he must do what good he could with the time left to him. And that would begin with laboring toward survival. He discarded his half-eaten chicken leg in a plastic-lined trash can, then shuffled to the beginning of the serving line, picked up plate, napkin, and silverware, and went from tray to tray, dishing up his dinner. Then he sat down on a stool near the cash register, and methodically set about eating as much of the meal as he could.

In spite of the fact that his stomach felt upset, and that he had so many fearful things with which to deal, his appetite returned with his first bite. The food tasted delicious to a man who hadn't eaten much in the past couple of days, but he found himself barely tasting it after he began shoveling it down. Oddly enough, his stomach settled down, and with each bite he felt strength returning to his body. *It must have been the drugs they gave me that upset my stomach,* he thought.

When he'd finished, he disposed of his paper napkin, then very carefully washed his plate and utensils. After he'd dried them and stacked them at the beginning of the serving line, he began to laugh at his behavior. Evidently old habits die hard. *On the other hand,* he thought, *of all the practices I must develop if I wish to survive, perhaps the first is cleanliness. I'm alone, and have no one to care for me. If at all possible, I must avoid sickness.* He shook his head slightly as though to clear his thoughts and organize his thinking. *And now, it's time to begin planning and preparing for the future.*

To that end, he found a dolly in the corner of the kitchen. After he filled a large cooking pot with fresh water and covered it with a lid, he began gathering canned goods and other items that would not quickly perish. He put them on the dolly, stacked on a garbage can and a quantity of trash bags, kitchen towels, and miscellaneous dishes and cutlery. He then pushed his load back to the X-ray room, leaning on the cart to keep from falling, moving slowly because of his pain and the intermittent vertigo.

As he was passing a bulletin board, he stopped to focus on a fund-raising announcement for an additional X-ray room. The poster featured an architectural rendering of the planned facility. This included structural details showing that the walls and ceiling were to be covered with a layer of lead a quarter-inch thick. He realized that the room in which he awoke, which he had initially despised, was a basement room with massive concrete walls, a steel-reinforced concrete ceiling, and on its interior walls, a lead lining. It was, in other words, one of America's best fallout shelters. Any room designed to keep radiation in would also keep radiation out. And the electrostatic filters that the hospital would have added to the air handlers to limit the spread of air borne diseases, and which were still undoubtedly being operated by the standby power system, would remove any radioactive dust from the air before it ever reached the X-ray room.

He had taken the radio from the kitchen, not realizing that it would be useless in that same lead-lined room. So he stripped the cords from several lamps, spliced them together, attached the wires to the radio's antenna, and taped it to the hallway wall outside the X-ray room door. After all that, he wasn't sure whether he'd solved the reception problem because he could no longer find any stations broadcasting.

He then rifled an infirmary for medical supplies. After that he took a mattress, blankets, sheets and a pillow from a storeroom, gathered some magazines, and made himself as comfortable as possible. He would look through the magazines later, he thought. Now he needed time. Time for his body to heal. Time for the war to resolve itself, and time for the outside air to clear sufficiently for him to leave the hospital. Most of all, he needed time to wait out the initial vicious half-lives of the deadly radiation. And, he thought, with more trepidation than hope, time to regain his memory. No matter what, he needed time to think and plan and prepare.

Although he was naturally troubled with a sense of disquiet, he put it down to the horrendous events occurring around him, not to any potential problems in his own past. There was nothing in him which was ready to lie down and die, no desire to quit. Whatever lay out there, he would start from this point and do the best he could.

Beneath the chair on which he'd discovered the wedding ring, he found a box containing some wrinkled underclothes. In a closet, he discovered a suit on a hanger and a pair of shoes. They fit him well, and he assumed they must be his. He picked up the ring and slipped it onto his finger. Somehow he felt more comfortable choosing one set of the initials, so he decided to adopt the first set. Until he could unravel this mystery, he would think of himself as "CC." Finding some non-prescription pain reliever, he took one, wrapped himself in the blankets, and finally fell asleep.

It hadn't yet occurred to him that the magazines he'd found would actually be repugnant. They were already impractical anachronisms, and would later remind him of the fool's paradise in which he'd lived, where people had not even considered the possibility of such events as these, let alone prepared themselves for them. The magazines, with their pictures of politicians, rock stars and actors, would have absolutely no practical value in his future.

And, he realized in surprising sadness, most of the people pictured in them, people who were envied by the average American, were very likely dead and had gone to a godless eternity. Many had probably never given serious consideration to their ultimate and eternal destiny, probably because they'd been taught that there is no life after death.

Back Bay Museum of Fine Art

Boston, Massachusetts
April 25th, 7:26 a.m.

Benton stared at her through bloodshot eyes, held out his bottle toward her, then changed his mind, tipping it up to take another swallow. He wiped his mouth with his sleeve, and said, "Everyone ran out of the building. They all wanted to get home to their families." He laughed hoarsely. "Except me. They didn't care about me, and I didn't care about them."

"What happened to the other employees?"

"I told you. They left the building." He rolled his eyes, a stupid grin on his face. "Just like Elvis." He laughed. Then he burped.

"Do you know what happened to them after they left the building?"

Another swallow. Another not quite sane laugh. “I doubt they made it to their cars before the shock wave hit.”

“What shock wave?”

“Must have been from a bomb,” he replied. “At least, I guess it was a bomb, a really big one.”

“What happened to you when this bomb went off?”

Now he seemed to sober a bit. “The last I remember, I was standing at the top of this staircase when a blast of air hit me and knocked me down. When I woke up, I was lying on the first landing. I must have been blown down an entire flight of stairs.” He did a sort of jig that left him standing with his back to her, and raised one hand, the bottle still in it, to point his index finger at the back of his head. “See?” he asked. His scalp was torn, and there was blood clotted in his hair, with large stains on his neck and shirt where the blood had run down.

Her growing fear of him caused her to stifle an impulse to offer to dress the wound for him. All she said was, “You're lucky it wasn't worse.”

“Yeah,” he answered indifferently. “When I woke up, I made my way back up to the reception area to see what was going on. I was alone, so I grabbed a few bottles from the hospitality room, and had a little party. Then I decided I should come down here and make sure you were all right.” He leered at her. “You look better than All right to me, baby.”

“I'm not your baby.”

His eyes seemed to roll backward; he caught the edge of a table to stabilize himself, and then he started shouting, “It's like the end of the world up there.”

She was concerned because one moment he'd seem rational, and the next, he acted like a lunatic. He repeated the statement several times, tears pouring from his eyes, “It's like the end of the world up there." He began to sway and again managed to catch the edge of a table. He looked like he was trying to force his eyes open, as though unable to focus. She imagined it was a combination of a concussion and the alcohol. He stared at her for a moment, seeming to comprehend who she was. He shook his head slowly from side to side. Then a sly smile replaced his look of confusion.

"We're alone, aren't we?" It wasn't a question.

"She didn't reply, but began to back casually toward the kitchenette. She hoped to shut and lock the door, but he staggered after her. Then he lowered his voice, clearly laboring to carefully pronounce his next words. "You know, Ross, we should work together to make the best of a bad situation."

Whitkowski Mushroom Caves

Lake Katrine, NY
April 25th, 7:35 p.m.

Eager to learn what was happening, Jonathan tested his portable radio, but when he pressed the search button, all he found was static. He had more success when he fastened the end of an insulated wire to the big door at the end of the tunnel, and ran it back into the cavern where he attached it to the antenna mounts on his radio.

At first, he operated it continuously, picking up any pieces of news he could get. Then, realizing that his store of batteries would run down quickly at this rate of usage, he forced himself to listen just a half hour each day. He found that he had much better reception in the middle of the night. There were almost no stations still broadcasting, but during the night he had been able to tune in to several AM stations that were thousands of miles away, some in foreign languages. He was sorry he hadn't worked harder in his French classes at school, and wished that he owned a ham radio rig, but, as an old friend used to say, "If wishes were fishes, we'd all live in the sea."

He had, nonetheless, learned that there had been at least six nuclear weapons detonated over the United States, and he realized that the actual number was probably far more. Information regarding the targets hit was difficult to obtain because there was little chance that any survivors would be on the air. One of the local Kingston stations had remained on the air for several days, broadcasting from the basement of a downtown office building. They affirmed the wisdom of his decision to hide in the cave. The radiation in his area of the mid-Hudson valley was heavy enough to be fatal for the first week, but he was encouraged that it might soon be possible to go outdoors for limited periods.

Each day, a sliver of sunlight shined through a crack between the doors at the front of the cave, and each day he used a garden tool to scratch a groove in the cave wall near the entrance to keep track of the date. Most of his time was spent back in his little room, what he'd come to call his "womb of the earth." Fortunately, he did not suffer from claustrophobia as he was forced to spend much of the time in the dark in order to conserve batteries. His one luxury was operating his LED flashlight for reading.

He realized he was gaining comfort from his Bible, a book he'd rarely turned to in the past. It was ironic, because he always considered it out of date and irrelevant. Now he realized that it was far more to the point than any contemporary book or magazine. He also spent a lot of time thumbing through an old encyclopedia, and reading books like "The Swiss Family Robinson," as well as other romanticized survival stories. When he'd finally scratched fourteen grooves on the cave wall, he hoped that the danger of radiation poisoning was past. He wanted to get outside into the sunlight.

Back Bay Museum of Fine Art

Boston, Massachusetts
April 25th, 7:42 a.m.

When Benton staggered to the kitchen table and dropped his heavy frame onto a tubular chair, Elizabeth gave a sigh of relief. He was still nursing the fifth of bourbon he'd carried down the stairs, but had occasionally held the bottle out, exhorting her in a slurred voice, "Have a little snort!"

After she'd repeatedly and politely refused, he carefully set the bottle on the table, his drunken movements exaggerated, then, when he was sure it wasn't going to tip over, he put his head down on his arms, and fell into a drunken stupor.

He began snoring loudly, but a moment later sat up abruptly, demanding to know where he was. His behavior was becoming increasingly erratic, and she was frightened. He leaned forward, obviously struggling to focus on her. He then started muttering, and finally pushed himself to his feet, swaying slightly, a bizarre smile on his face, his eyes fixed on her body.

He suddenly fell to his knees, but it proved a feint, for as he fell, he lunged for her. She just managed to scurry out of his reach. Using a chair to pull himself to his feet, he began to stalk her as she backed around the room. "You and me," he began mumbling repeatedly.

"You and me, what?" she asked.

He rolled his head back and forth, a bizarre smile on his face. "You know! You and me," and he hiccuped.

"What about your wife," she asked to gain time, hoping he might pass out again.

"What about her?" he countered. "We're divorced now. I can't get to her, and she can't get to me, and I couldn't be a happier man."

She had backed into the refrigerator. Slipping past it, she opened the door and grabbed the first thing she put her hands on, a foil-covered tray of sandwiches. "Here," she said, "how about something to eat?"

"Maybe later," he replied, as he pushed the tray aside. She tried to catch it as it fell to the floor, but he took advantage of her confusion to grab one of her arms. She pushed him away, and he slipped and fell. Now he was both angry and demanding, and began to threaten her. While he was getting back on his feet, she scrambled through the work room door, slamming and locking it behind her.

A moment later he began pounding on the door, screaming obscenities. When she realized he couldn't get in, her breathing became more regular, and she was able to begin thinking rationally. After a couple of minutes she was relieved but also a bit frightened that his frustrated hammering had stopped.

She knew that he had to be looking for a way into the work room. She ran across the floor and, just in time, slammed and locked the door to the main room. Then it occurred to her that all he needed to do was push a table up against the ten foot partition separating the two rooms, set a chair on it, climb up on the chair, push a section of the suspended ceiling out of the way, climb over the top of the partition, and drop to the workroom floor.

When she heard a table being slid across the floor, she feared that he had been reading her mind. She moved toward the door so that she could run back into the kitchen if he came over the wall into the work room. When there was no sound of him climbing onto the table or moving the ceiling panels, she realized that this evidently wasn't his plan.

She didn't want to hurt him, but he'd made it clear what he intended to do to her. He was acting like a crazy man, and she felt that she had to take measures to defend herself, so she began frantically searching for something to use as a weapon. *My word*, she thought, *he must be twice my size.*

She moved to the huge felt-top work table in the center of the room. The first things she noticed was an unusually large and heavy pair of scissors, perhaps fourteen inches long. They had sharply pointed blades, designed for making neat straight cuts. She caught them up, wondering whether she'd be able to use them as a knife, and questioning whether she could bring herself to use them at all. Then she realized that, with his superior size and strength, he would probably wrest them away from her and maybe even use them on her. She dropped them back on the table, and began searching for a better weapon.

She hoped to find something like a baseball bat, but the heaviest thing she could locate was a broom. She immediately rejected that because it was too light-weight, and he'd easily wrest it from her. She again examined the scissors. *If nothing else comes to hand, the scissors will have to be my Plan B,* she thought. Then she realized that she had no Plan A.

There is no baseball bat, she realized. Maybe at Fenway

Park, but not in the Back Bay Art Museum. Not where I need it.

As she began dragging the large sheets of brown wrapping paper from the table top to the floor in order to see what else might be laying on the table, she heard a tremendous crash. It shook the entire wall. Her heart seemed to stop, and when she got control of herself, she could hear him outside the door laughing hysterically.

"We'll get her now, Benton," he was chanting quietly to himself. "We'll get her now." He began bragging to himself how he would take down the door using his home-made battering ram.

It took all her strength, but she pushed the work table up against the door to try to keep him from breaking through. Then she set a chair on the table, and climbed up so that she could pop a ceiling tile loose. The tile fell to the floor near his feet, and he looked up at her.

"Clever idea," he chortled. Why didn't I think of that?" He staggered to the kitchen counter and took another drink from his bottle. Then he shook the bottle, and when he didn't hear any liquid splash, he held it up to his eye to see whether there was any liquor left. Angry that it was empty, he reached back and threw it, striking the wall a few feet below her.

"You throw like a girl," she joked, and realized immediately that she should have kept her silence.

He roared like a wounded bull, and staggered back across the room to the dining table which he'd tipped up on one edge, its legs now parallel to the floor. Furious at her for mocking him, he began sliding it across the polished floor toward the connecting door, using it as a battering ram. He missed the door, but the end of the table slammed so hard against the frame that it shook the entire wall, and actually bounced the table she was standing on.

She immediately stepped down from the chair, then jumped from the table to the floor, shaking with terror. *There's no question about the ethics of defending myself,* she realized. *There's only a question of the feasibility.* A full minute passed, her mind struggling with her seemingly insoluble dilemma. The table slammed into the door again, and she saw the door's metal surface bounce under the impact. That time he'd definitely hit the door. She wondered how much more it could stand.

She picked up a chair, but realized it was too heavy for her to wield against him. He would easily snatch it from her. Unfortunately, he wouldn't hit her with it until he'd satisfied his lusts. *What else is there?* she wondered. There has to be something else. She looked for the scissors on the floor, and noticed that they had opened into a big X where she'd dropped them. They had fallen atop the end of a long stainless steel yard stick, a tool ordinarily used as a guide to trim hard board with a knife.

Where the open scissors crossed the end of the yardstick, they looked a little like a crucifix. One handle rested on the top of the yard stick, its blade pointing up, like the point of a spear. The other handle pointed off to the left, with its blade pointing in the opposite direction, like the cross member on which Christ's hands were nailed.

It seemed odd to her, at that moment, that she would be asking herself whether he had died for her. Then she saw the open scissors as something else.

"Will it work?" she wondered aloud.

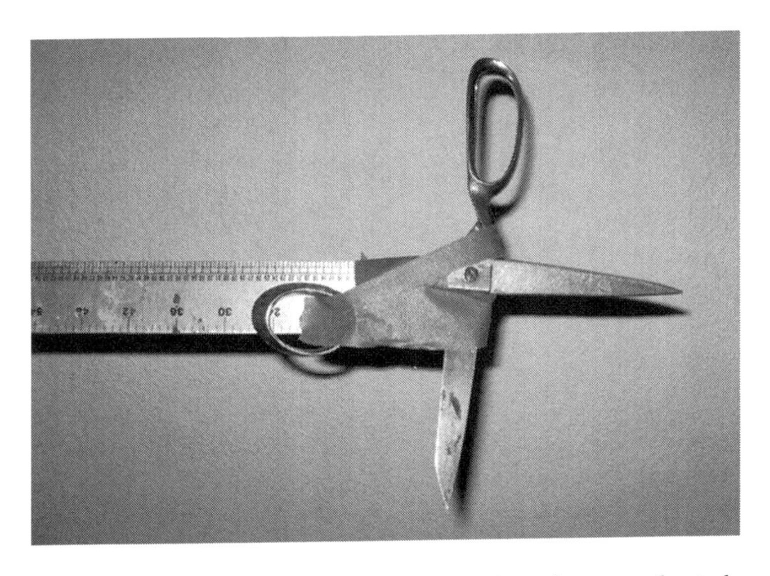

She dropped a roll of fiberglass-reinforced tape and cried out in terror as Benton's makeshift battering ram again struck the door. Turning to look, she saw that a narrow crack had opened between the door and the casing on one side. *Not much time left,* she realized.

She grabbed the tape dispenser and began winding the wide reinforced tape across the screw where the scissor handles met the blades, then around the tip of the steel yardstick, and back around the scissors, back and forth, crisscrossing the scissors and the steel yardstick, around and around, until the open scissors seemed solidly secured to the last six inches of the yardstick. Then she wrapped her hands around the center of the yardstick, picked it up, and shook it hard.

In spite of the violent motion, the scissors remained fixed to the end of the yardstick, one blade pointing straight forward off the end like a spear, the other at a right angle. It reminded her of the ancient war axes that the knights of old had wielded, weapons she'd paid scant attention to in the medieval museums she'd visited in Europe.

The sharp edges of the yardstick hurt her hands, so she found a matching yardstick on a desk, and began taping it alongside the first. This both thickened and stiffened her "axe handle" and provided a better grip.

The table slammed into the door behind her, bringing her out of her musings and back to reality. She realized that sound was different. Instead of a ringing blow, there was a duller crunching sound, as though the solid liner of the door was splitting apart. She turned to look and saw that the door frame had broken loose, and the bottom corner of the door was twisted wide open. She could see Benton leering at her through the opening as he lay down on the floor to crawl through the opening.

She should have attacked him then, while he was relatively helpless, but felt frozen in place. He crawled into the room on his side, a wolfish smile on his face, curses passing his lips. Then he rose to his feet.

"No more threats," he said. "Now you both play and pay," he promised, and even if she were not warned by the insanity in his eyes, she would have been by the light flashing off the carving knife he gripped in his hand.

She had been momentarily hidden from his view as he crawled into the room, and she quickly unfastened the two top buttons of her blouse. It offered only a slight view of her cleavage, but it was enough to draw his drunken gaze away from her hands.

"Ah, so now you want to play, do you?" he asked, leering at

her. "Well, maybe I won't need this after all," he said, waving the carving knife so wildly that he almost cut his own face.

She was leaning over the high work table where she'd left her improvised battle ax lying flat on its baize surface. His eyes were fixed on her, but even if he had looked down at the table, it was unlikely that he would have discerned her purpose, nor would he have noticed that her hands now gripped the yardstick. His feverish eyes were fixed on other things, and he was certain that he had her where he wanted her.

He wheeled around the end of the table. As he lunged at her, she was filled with a sense of horror, and swung to face him. And as she turned, the improvised battle ax, which in her terror she'd forgotten was locked in her hands, swung in a wide arc. His eyes caught the light flashing off her makeshift weapon, but he had already heaved himself forward to grab her.

Suddenly realizing his danger, he dropped the knife in order to reach out to protect himself, and the point of the scissor blade drove through the palm of his hand. He shrieked with the pain, then raised his other fist to strike her. She pulled on the yardsticks, trying to back away, but the muscles and tendons in his hand seemed to grip the scissor blade. He screamed again, then punched her hard in the mouth.

She stumbled back a step, nearly blacking out with the shock and pain, but she somehow held doggedly to the yardstick with one hand. The point of the "axe" was still embedded in his hand. Again grasping the yardsticks with both hands, she stepped to her left, trying to keep the point of the weapon, the spear point that had impaled his hand, between them, and attempting to take advantage of the length of the yardstick to keep him from punching her again.

He screamed repeatedly as their uncoordinated movements caused the blade to twist in his hand.

That twisting, as agonizing as it was for him, finally freed the blade, and he yanked his hand away, holding it to his belly, the blood flowing copiously as it soaked into his shirt and dripped to the floor. His expression changed. Desire had turned to malice.

"I'm going to kill you," he promised, and the threat was all the more menacing because it was said with such quiet conviction. Then, with a certain cunning in his voice, he revealed his true feelings. "There's really not enough food here for both of us anyway."

He backed away, found a cloth dishtowel by the sink, and wrapped it around his injured hand, trying clumsily to tie a knot using his teeth and his left hand. He moved toward an old-fashioned metal trash can in the corner. The museum workers used it to store rags that had been soaked with turpentine and paint in order to guard against fire. He lifted the lid with his left hand, and gripping its handle, held it in front of him, like a shield.

He bent to pick up the broom to use as a club, but his wounded right hand was now useless. Nonetheless, he rushed her, hoping to beat her with the metal cover, believing his brute strength sufficient to overwhelm her.

In this, she was in terrified agreement, but because the alcohol had left him with poor coordination, she was able to shift to her side and avoid this second assault which saw him slam into the edge of the work table. She now realized that her situation was nearly hopeless, but wasn't about to give up. *If I'm going down,* she thought, *I'm going to make a fight of it.*

Holding the yardstick before her in both hands, like a short spear, she again backed away from him. In an attempt to disarm her, he uttered a loud roar, and again rushed her, holding the metal garbage can lid by it's handle, using it to protect his chest, planning perhaps to club her with it. He struck the end of her makeshift spear hard with the lid, hoping to force the tip of the blade to penetrate its surface, to capture it the way his hand had earlier gripped it, perhaps to twist it away from her. But things didn't work out the way he'd planned.

His makeshift shield tipped, the spear point slid under its lower edge, and drove under his belt, penetrating several inches into his lower abdomen. He stopped in his tracks, his eyes wide with disbelief. For a moment, he stood perfectly still. Then, without a word, he dropped to his knees, the trash can lid slipping from his hand and rolling noisily across the room.

Looking down, he moaned with terror when he saw the scissor blade buried in his groin area. His hands scrabbled at the yard stick. Then he rolled onto his side. Blood was pouring from both the grievous wound in his abdomen and from his hand. Grasping the yardstick with his undamaged hand, he tried futilely to withdraw it, but the movement was obviously excruciating, and he immediately relaxed his grip. After a moment, he tried again, and the blade slipped free, followed by a gout of blood and other dark body fluids. Looking up into her eyes, his lips twisted into a grotesque smile. He tried to mouth some words, but there was only a guttural sigh. Then, after a few minutes that seemed like a lifetime to Elizabeth, he shuddered, and all movement ceased.

She ran from the room, dropped to the floor, and was violently ill. After a while, she returned to the room. He lay motionless, his face now white from loss of blood.

Although she covered his body with a couple of the

caterer's paper table cloths, it became clear by the second day ×
that something had to be done. The vault had a specially filtered ventilation system to ground level, but it wouldn't keep the air in the vault from being polluted from within. So she looked for a place that she could put his body where decomposition wouldn't be a danger to her.

After rejecting the elevator and stair case, she thought of ×
the special room where the museum stored particularly fragile and valuable artworks. Before she opened its airtight door, she pumped the inert gas out, replacing it with air. It took all of her strength to drag Benton's body over the threshold and into the vault. Closing the door, she again recharged the room with the inert gas. Her eyes flooded with tears as she tried to convince herself that his death was necessary. It was, nonetheless, a relief to have his remains out of sight, if not out of mind.

Medical Center

Deep River Junction, Vermont
April 25th, 3 p.m.

After fighting with indecision, CC left the X-ray room, and began climbing the stairway to the upper stories. There was no sign of life on the main floor. The information booth was vacant, the halls silent. When he cracked the door to the floor above, he was struck with the stench of death. He returned to the basement, and decided to look around outside.

No matter where he went in the community, that stench was pervasive, and often overpowering. Wearing a surgical mask helped some, for it reduced both the unspeakable odors as well as the possibility of inhaling anything infectious.

Next door to the hospital was a small chain grocer. Just two weeks after the holocaust, the supermarket, that marvel of America's merchandising skills, was no longer a fit place to enter. Nor was such an effort profitable, for the "shopper" was more apt to be attacked by rats or infected with disease than to find edible food. CC suspected this, and a quick glance through the broken glass doors confirmed his worst fears. The place had been ransacked. And it was clearly unfit, perhaps even dangerous, to enter.

The business district proved the least unpleasant, obviously because most people had deserted the area upon learning of the attack. He was forced to avoid residential areas. The terrible odors that pervaded the air made it obvious that most of those who had left their work places and schools had returned to their homes, only to perish there. Few realized that the fallout from nuclear weapons, even though detonated thousands of miles away, might land on their homes. Nor were they aware that the invisible and deadly gamma rays would penetrate their roofs and walls to invade their bodies.

CC had learned a great deal about the horrors of radiation poisoning while he was waiting out his two weeks in the X-ray room. As his strength had returned, he had spent much of his time preparing for the trials that he knew lay ahead. He considered that, realistically, the odds of his survival were extremely low. So he determined to prepare himself, mentally, physically, and spiritually, and he began by slowing down.

He opened his Bible to the Proverbs, and sought wisdom for his preparations. The one thing he came away with was the certainty that he must take measures to assist others whom he might meet along the way. When he began preparing lists of things to do as well as items it would be desirable to acquire, he tried to keep that in mind.

He found that instead of lying around, he was working longer days. To strengthen his body, he ate carefully prepared meals using the healthiest foods that remained in the hospital kitchen. And he jogged up and down the basement hallways for a half hour every day after completing a number of calisthenics. Then he discovered a small gym in the far corner of the basement that had been reserved for doctors and nurses, and he began weight training.

To develop mentally, he focused on the things he needed to know in order to survive in a post-nuclear environment, and a world almost certainly gripped by anarchy. He made frequent trips to the basement library in order to get answers to his questions. It was on the third day that he noticed a beeping noise coming from one office, and discovered that the hospital computer system was still up. Lifting the wrist rest that lay in front of the keyboard, he found the former user's ID and password written on a scrap of paper that was taped to the desk top.

The Internet was down, so he could not access the outside world, but he learned a great deal from the hospital's database. It consisted not merely of staff and patient data, but also stored a great deal of information from Homeland Security and the CDC, as well as other organizations that dealt with emergency preparedness and medical care. He used the office laser printer to copy anything that appeared to be of value. Placing these sheets in a loose-leaf binder, he spent hours exhaustively studying them, attempting to adapt the information, much of it theoretical, to the challenge of his own long-term survival.

First, of course, there was the danger from the fallout

itself. Charts and tables showed the hazards from various levels of radiation produced by different radioactive isotopes. This information was of passing interest, but essentially useless because there would be no one available to tell him which elements were present, and in what quantity and intensity.

Questions like how far away the bombs had exploded, and how much fallout had dropped out of the atmosphere, were also time-wasters, as were questions like, had the bomb or bombs been detonated thousands of feet in the air in order to increase their explosive effect, or had they been detonated near the ground, so that they would scoop up and contaminate thousands of tons of earth. All this had little meaning, except to suggest that the clouds of contaminants might be dropping out of the sky for years rather than months.

One sobering question involved the half-life of the fissionable material, the stuff that made the bomb go "boom," and produced the deadly radiation. Under the most desirable circumstances, relatively few of the estimated 50,000 nuclear warheads around the world would have been detonated. He learned that fallout generated by an explosion anywhere else in the world might sooner or later come his way because of the high altitude winds. A bomb set off in San Francisco might well poison the soil in Kansas City, unless rain storms or errant winds caused the residue to drop to the earth before reaching there.

He learned that fallout, and the gasses generated by nuclear detonations, could reach high into the stratosphere where they would create all sorts of problems. They might prevent sunlight from reaching parts of the earth, as well as disturb normal wind, snow, and rainfall patterns. They could change summer to winter, and turn fertile lands to deserts.

Depending on various factors, those winds might sweep in huge Omega-shaped pockets (Ω) toward the equator, and over months or even years unload much of their lethal radioactive fallout in that belt that runs around the earth's equator between the Tropic of Cancer and the Tropic of Capricorn. That belt takes in most of Africa, much of South America, all of India, Southeast Asia, and the northern half of Australia.

Since presumably most missiles would be detonated in the northern hemisphere—over North America, Europe, and Asia—a good deal of the fallout would initially fall out over these land masses. Nevertheless, no matter where it fell, it would probably be a lose-lose situation for everyone on earth. Just as weather patterns are disturbed after a major volcanic eruption, so it could be presumed that multiple nuclear explosions would result in global cooling, as the gasses produced would block the sunlight. And if the winds moved north and south toward the polar ice caps, then most of the more dangerous detritus would drop out over places like Canada, Alaska, and Siberia in the north, and Australia, Argentina, and the south Pacific islands in the south.

It wouldn't really matter where it fell, it would again be a lose-lose situation. The fallout itself would kill countless people and livestock, and pollute crops. After that, worldwide famine would likely ensue because the temperature of the atmosphere would only have to drop a degree or two to wipe out crops needed to feed those populations and their livestock.

As CC read on, he became increasingly negative, not

merely for himself, or even for any loved ones that might still be alive somewhere, but for the entire human race.

With every added mile of distance from ground zero, a person's chances of survival would theoretically improve. It was theoretical because survival would depend on how the winds blew, not just the winds we feel at the earth's surface, but especially those that are a hundred thousand feet above us. If a five-megaton bomb exploded on the earth's surface, it might vaporize and pulverize a million tons of earth, radiating it, and carrying it into the stratosphere.

Ever since the Chernobyl nuclear power plant in the Ukraine had begun melting down, winds had been carrying the radioactive fallout it produced in a northwest direction across Europe and out over the Atlantic to North America. The impact was so severe that in many northern European countries the toxic material has entered the water supply and the food chain.

Even for those fortunate enough to be well away from the epicenter of the blast, it would still be a matter of the quantity and intensity of the radioactive elements that made up the "fallout" that fell on them, almost like an invisible and deadly snow storm. Its presence might be suspected if one saw dust falling from the sky, or rain that left a dark residue. Otherwise it would be detected in one of two ways, either with a radiation detector, or by how it was manifested. If it were fairly light, then humans and animals might survive for years, but their immune systems would be damaged, and they would be prone to all sorts of ailments from tooth decay to terminal cancer.

Apart from the deaths directly resulting from the nuclear attacks, those anticipated changes in weather patterns could be devastating. During the 19th Century, one volcanic eruption in the Pacific had resulted in a drop in temperatures of about 1 degree that destroyed crops in much of the world, and resulted in massive starvation. With the starvation that would follow this war, CC wouldn't be surprised if less than a quarter of the world's population survived.

He realized that, in order to survive, he would need to accomplish one of three things. The most desirable would be to discover and safely move to a location where there was no fallout, a highly unlikely possibility. Next would be to find a location where the decay of the radioactive material would render it relatively harmless in a short period, say a couple of weeks. Even under those circumstances, he would need to remain sheltered until any residue lost its potency. Or, finally, he would need to shelter indefinitely, probably underground —a virtual impossibility. The alternative to these might be an agonizing death.

Assuming he could find such a place, there would still be the problem of providing food, shelter, clothing, and medical care over the long term, and protecting himself from others who might covet his advantages.

Initially, CC needed to know how much fallout had already dropped out of the sky in whatever location he would be attempting to survive, and how long that fallout would remain dangerous? Since he was unlikely to be able to travel far, that probably meant central Vermont.

The experts measure the "decay" of radioactive materials in what they call "half-lives." If the radioactivity had a half-life of two weeks, then it would lose half its deadly energy in two weeks, and half of its remaining energy in the two weeks that followed. So by the end of six weeks, it would be emitting only about an eighth of its initial radiation. But if the isotope's half-life was not merely two weeks, but say a thousand years, then it would take thousands of years before it was at an eighth of its initial strength. And it might be many thousands of years before anyone could live where that fallout lay on the ground in any measurable quantity. Hopefully the bombs that were detonated were composed of radioactive material that was relatively short-lived.

Practically speaking, it came down to a simple formula. If he detected any radiation, he must either shield himself from it, a near impossibility, or get away from it, perhaps equally impossible. He'd need equipment to detect any radiation, and he'd have to hope that he could locate a place where the levels were extremely low. So, number one on his list was some kind of radiation detector. In that respect, he couldn't have found himself in a more opportune place. The radiological department at this hospital had all sorts of equipment on hand to check for safe levels of radiation.

Next, at least for the first few weeks, he'd need to limit the quantities of dust he might breath or ingest in food and water. Wearing even a nuisance dust mask would help with the breathing. Eating from cans and bottles that had not been irradiated would promote the other. Shaving his head, taking frequent showers, and washing his clothes daily, would help prevent fallout from clinging to his body.

It seemed simple to him. He must be very careful, he realized, but if the radiation proved widespread, intense, and prolonged, all the care in the world wouldn't make any difference. He'd have to remain in this lead-lined X-ray room until he ran out of food and water, and then he would perish. These conclusion resulted in his doing a little wool-gathering.

How many Americans, I wonder, will survive this catastrophe? Not necessarily those who are especially intelligent or physically strong. And not necessarily even those who had prepared for disaster. Even many of the survivalists, those who invested much of their time and money in preparing for disaster, may have perished. In spite of all their careful preparations, they might have found themselves hundreds of miles away from their shelters on business or pleasure.

His thoughts raced on. *Those who would try to exploit others, killing and looting, would sooner or later discover that the remaining stores of foods and medicines would be exhausted or spoiled, or in the hands of well-armed groups. Survivors,* he reasoned, *will include those who prepared themselves mentally and spiritually for any situation in life, individuals with a strong will to live, imaginative and flexible, particularly those who understood that they have a God who cares for them.*

He understood one thing, those who survived should not simply be strong, but should possess the kind of character required to rebuild the nation.

"There I go again, wool-gathering," he said aloud. "I've got to stay focused!" As he returned to the tasks at hand, he realized that he had an enormous advantage over most people facing these problems, and that he could take absolutely no credit for any of it.

He'd been in an auto accident, which seemed like a bad thing. And he'd wound up unconscious, alone, and with amnesia, in the basement of a hospital, which also seemed like a bad thing. He had, in fact, been blessed with an incredible variety of the resources that would promote his survival. Under the circumstances, it would be difficult for him to deny that there was a loving personality watching over him. *But why me?* he wondered.

The X-ray department had lead aprons and other gear to protect patients and staff from excess radiation. In addition, there were various devices to measure the amount of radiation exposure, both its intensity and the amount absorbed over a given period. These included the badges that technicians would be required to wear to make certain they were not dangerously overexposed.

The first time CC went outdoors, just a week after the nuclear warheads had struck, it was to rush out into the courtyard to hang one of those detection badges on the branch of a forsythia bush. He remained outside only long enough to accomplish that task. He could scarcely move because of the weight of the lead aprons he'd wrapped around his body and draped over his head. And when he checked the badge an hour later, it indicated a high level of radiation. He'd check it again in a few days. A lower level would provide an indication of how rapidly it was diminishing.

At the end of the second week, he put a fresh badge outside. After the allotted hour, he was delighted to see that it was virtually unchanged. He nevertheless decided to remain inside for two more days. He realized, of course, that when he began moving about outside, he would find "hot spots" here and there, locations where radiation was greater because wind or rain had caused the fallout to collect in that area.

He'd have to continually monitor his detection equipment as he moved from place to place. He'd found several dosimeters and Geiger counters that would help him do so. They would warn him of any danger by clicking loudly or even "speaking" with a robotic voice. One device had a GPS built in, and provided both latitude and longitude, thus enabling him to mark on a map the precise areas of great danger or safety.

His next question was, *How many people will I be competing with for food, shelter, and other necessities of life?* He realized that many survivors would be very dangerous individuals who would stop at nothing to stay alive. Under these circumstances, the survival of the fittest, or of the nastiest, would rule the day. He must somehow avoid contact with such people, and he must be prepared to defend himself.

Will I he be able to find any food supplies or water that will be safe to eat and drink, and even if I do, will I find enough to keep me alive for any meaningful period? And if, by some stretch of the imagination, all the answers to these other questions are acceptable, what's the point of surviving in the short-term if I cannot sustain a life that's worth living over the long-term?

How could anyone, he wondered, *build a life in a world without electricity, gasoline, super-markets, medical care, and police protection? And even if I find food, clothing, and other items that would sustain me for several months, or even years, sooner or later, I'll have to be able to provide those things for myself.*

He realized that he'd have to grow, harvest, and store his own food. How primitive, he wondered, would his lifestyle have to become in order for him to be able to sustain it? And without having others around to assist him—people to share the burdens, to provide expertise, and help one another through times of sickness, accident and even loneliness—how would anyone survive? Wouldn't he go nuts living as a hermit?

And what about my family, he wondered. *I must have had a family. Is there a possibility that they've survived? Will I ever see them again?* Somehow it was painful to consider this possibility, and he found himself continually turning away from the thought. He determined to consciously force his thoughts away from any unprofitable or negative line of thinking. *I simply must not worry about things over which I have no control. They sap my energy and ruin my focus.*

A more practical question intruded. If he found anyone with whom he might attempt to share his life, to what standard of living would they have to sink in order to survive? Must they live like the early pioneers? Would they have to revert to being cavemen? And how would they protect themselves against enemies who were intent on exploiting or killing them?

Yet, even as he asked himself those questions, he realized that he wouldn't give up trying no matter how unpleasant things became. And he also realized that there were probably many survivors who had asked themselves those same questions, and some of them would already have given up in despair, and because they'd given up, they'd perished.

During his first few days in the X-ray room, he'd concentrated on eating, sleeping, and regaining his strength. In the cafeteria, he put all the spoiled food into plastic bags and put the bags in covered trash cans. Then he washed everything. He wasn't surprised that there was an abundance of water. The tank on the roof of the hospital probably held thousands of gallons.

The supply of hot water surprised him until he located the mechanical room and discovered that the hospital heated its water with fuel oil. Since the furnaces and water heaters continued to receive the relatively small amount of electrical power they required from the generator, he would enjoy the luxury of hot baths for a while longer.

It took him several hours to clean up the kitchen, but he felt a lot better about preparing food in a clean environment. The other thing that initially surprised him was that both the walk-in freezer and the walk-in cooler were operating, and he was able to prepare dinners of steak and seafood, including vegetables. He could even have fruit or ice cream whenever he wanted it, though he knew this wouldn't go on for long.

Medical Center

Deep River Junction, Vermont
April 26th, 9 a.m.

Before CC had discovered the hospital's computer data base, he'd taken a wheeled cart to the library and brought back scores of books that he stacked along the walls of the X-ray room. The library at the hospital was larger than he'd expected, and contained a number of books which were to prove profitable, and from which he took copious notes.

Sometimes he tore pages from the books or magazines so that he could reduce the material to manageable bits of useful information, and he organized these in binders. For the first time in his life, he found himself studying books on first-aid, human anatomy, and even surgery.

He found a phone book, and tore out listings for local distributors of products and services which he thought he would need. These included grocery wholesalers, lumber yards, hardware stores, electronics firms, and sporting goods suppliers. Most major suppliers listed in the book were located in distant cities, but he found several small local wholesalers. Most importantly, there were two competing home improvement centers in the town.

The only question was, *Would these places already be stripped bare when he got to them?* In spite of his concerns about the availability of items he might require, he refused to risk leaving the hospital prematurely. He was not willing to risk cancer and other debilitating and fatal illnesses by going outside before the radiation had been reduced to an acceptable level.

He would have to plan these little forays carefully, for the world had changed dramatically. Through the twenty-first century, it had been continually shrinking. Just a month before, a traveler could have flown nearly anywhere in twenty-four hours. People had viewed live TV broadcasts beamed by satellite from distant lands. With the advent of war, however, the world had grown again. The progress in travel and communications that had required centuries to develop had been wiped out, virtually overnight. There were probably very few passenger jets in the air, or ships sailing the seas.

Now a person's world was pretty much limited to the distance that he could walk in half a day, because it would be necessary to return to shelter by evening. And now the human race would have to revert to the use of a compass and map, because the satellites that carried signals for global positioning systems were probably no longer in service. And even if they were, the means to recharge batteries was gone.

CC knew that he must become self-sufficient, or as nearly so as his strength and skill would permit. In a world which had become increasingly specialized, one in which people had relied more and more on packaged retail goods and the sophisticated electronics and transportation systems to deliver them, he was on his own. Their would be no more smart phones, electronic book readers, laptop computers, internet, or overnight deliveries.

First of all, he must stay healthy to remain alive. Any failure to sustain himself under all circumstances, at all times, would ultimately result in his death. Prior to the war, America had evolved into a society dining on microwave meals and fast-food lunches. Restaurants that served all manner of delicacies at a wide variety of prices had become ubiquitous, but that too was a thing of the past. Now he would have to become independent, with the necessity of growing, processing, and preserving his own food, just as his forefathers had.

And he would not have high-tech equipment or gasoline-powered engines to achieve this goal. If he traveled, he would have to carry his shelter and bed on his back, along with sufficient food and safe water to provide for the entire journey.

During the two weeks he remained at the hospital, he tried to develop a long-term plan that would provide some of the benefits of the lifestyle he had known. As long as gasoline was available for a chain saw and other tools, he could accomplish a lot with relatively little labor, but as time went on, without access to petroleum products and electricity, he knew his survival would conform to the labor-intensive environment of the pre-industrial age.

He was faced with the challenge of providing a palatable, healthy diet, as well as clothing, health and hygiene supplies, some means of transportation, and much more. He would require a reliable source of pure water, as well as a waste-water system, both conveniences that he formerly took for granted. Suddenly something as mundane as a working toilet, and the tissue to go with it, would become inconceivable luxuries. He'd have little spare time for entertainment and education, even if the means were still available. Above all, he needed a secure and functional shelter, as well as a means to heat it.

He realized that he would have to make a careful selection of the tools and equipment that might be available to him, knowing that he would never again be able to go to a nearby mall to pick up a needed item. What's more, even if he were to go foraging in the future, there was a question as to whether he'd find anything in the stores, let alone be able to safely return to his home. Others would almost certainly be raiding those same resources, if they had not already done so. And now, to complicate matters even further, America had been invaded by at least two foreign powers intent on taking control.

Nor could he count on government or industry to restore the infrastructure in the foreseeable future. The blackout in the northeast U.S. during the early 1960s demonstrated how fragile the infrastructure was. In the half a century since that blackout, things had grown far worse. The impact of a single hurricane, a Mississippi flood, or a terrorist bombing inevitably resulted in both economic and emotional depression. Even bridges judged to be safe had unexpectedly collapsed.

And with the nation's resources stretched thin, with taxes and deficits rising, and with a plethora of exigent socialist politicians in control, the equitable distribution of resources and rewards had vanished. The emergencies that America had faced in the past were nothing compared with the catastrophe that had resulted from the detonation of numerous nuclear weapons. Whatever remained of society, he realized, would be in a state of indescribable chaos.

Somehow, he determined, I've got to secure and sustain an acceptable level of living indefinitely without returning to a stone-age mentality. From there I might again locate my family or offer assistance to a few others.

This meant that he had to be able to secure the tools he'd need to make clothing, to grow and prepare food, to heat his home, and to defend it against predators. Depression threatened to overwhelm him until he spent time in prayer.

Underworld Caverns

Utica, New York
May 6th, 7:45 a.m.

Rachel had plenty of opportunity to read the survival manuals that she found among the civil defense supplies. Following their suggested guidelines, she sheltered there for what she hoped would be a minimum safe period, and then climbed the eighteen-story staircase to ground level.

Just before she reached the surface, she opened a side door onto another stairway that led to the gift shop and snack bar. She used the radiation detector to make sure that levels were safe. Noticing a door marked "Fallout Shelter," she smiled, confident that she'd find some survivors with whom she could discuss her next steps.

When she opened the door, however, she was greeted with a horrible scene. In the near darkness she could see bodies all over the place. The odor was horrible, and she slammed the door on the scene, then fell to her knees and was violently ill. When she was again in control of herself, she rose to her feet and climbed the stairs toward the snack bar. *They'd have been a lot better off to stay down below where I was,* she realized.

There was sunlight coming in through the clerestory windows in the gift shop, and she again checked for radiation. She was happy to discover that the levels were normal, and that she could safely exit the building. The first thing she took from a shelf was a small, exorbitantly priced bottle of mouthwash, and she immediately used it. When she found a stack of toothbrushes, small tubes of toothpaste, and a bottle of drinking water, she brushed her teeth for the first time in over two weeks.

Then she sat down on the floor, leaned against the wall, and cried her heart out. After being alone for two weeks, then finding all those people dead, she realized that she really was on her own. That one realization, that a person can be completely and totally alone, was devastating.

It was decision time. She had to settle the question of whether she was going to acquiesce to circumstance and just let go, or do what she must do to survive. For Rachel, it had never really been an issue.

She found a cardboard carton, filled it with snacks and bottled beverages, grabbed a spoon, a can opener, two butane lighters, and several small flashlights from a display card, and started back down the stairs to the caverns. She rinsed all of the bottles and cans off in the underground river. The relatively fresh canned goods were a great replacement for the flat tasting old food in the lower shelter.

She realized that most people had no idea how to react in an emergency. Few are ever prepared. It's certainly wasn't her fault that others made wrong choices, but whatever motivated her to stay down in that cavern during and after the attack was certainly providential.

Her perspective changed, and though she wondered whether her fiancee might still be alive, it no longer mattered. Since she was alone, she had to bear her own burdens. She hesitated for a moment. *No, that's wrong,* she thought. T*here is another person here.* And she smiled to herself as she looked up and whispered softly, "Thank you, Lord." With wonder in her voice she acknowledged, "My survival is really your miracle."

She stayed in the fallout shelter two additional days, just to play it safe, but she got to the point that she couldn't stand it any more. She felt as though the walls were closing in on her, and she just had to get out of the place.

The boats had been washed away in the flooding, so she carried what she could down to the end of the walkway, then waded out through the shallow stream to the dam. Her legs were freezing, and she sat on that little dam and tried to rub some warmth back into her feet. On the downstream side of the dam, she resumed her wading through the much shallower water, and after about a quarter-mile, she reached a huge drain pipe that had been installed to shore up the crust of the mountain where it drained the caverns.

When she stepped out of the tunnel into daylight, she found herself at the bottom of a huge stone quarry. The quarry had high walls on three sides from which they'd blasted the stone. The fourth side was open, and faced south, where the stream drained into the Mohawk Valley.

That night she slept in the concrete office building that was located alongside the quarry's main road. There was a pickup truck parked outside the office. The door of the office had been left wide open, and she found the keys to the truck in a desk drawer. There was a gasoline storage tank with a hand crank pump on top. She filled the truck's tank, plus some spare cans she found in a shed.

There was a blanket on a sofa in the office, and she grabbed that. She pulled the thumbtacks that secured a map of New York to the office wall, folded it, and added it to her treasures. Then she searched through the place taking anything that might be of value.

When she'd loaded everything in the truck, she headed north on back roads. Later that day she drove through a hamlet, found an abandoned gas station and convenience store, and loaded the bed of the truck with canned goods and beverages. Staying clear of the state capital and going east across the Hudson River would be problematic. She consulted her map, and continued following rural roads north until she found a bridge that crossed the Mohawk River near Saratoga. She then worked her way east toward Vermont.

Medical Center

Deep River Junction, Vermont
May 6th, 8 a.m.

On the sixteenth day, CC reviewed his notes, then walked to the city's truck dealer where he found a brand new ten-wheel tractor and trailer combination.

There was paper work on the driver's seat indicating that it had been scheduled to be delivered to its new owner the day after the war started. The keys had been left over the visor. Unfortunately, its fuel tank was only about an eighth full. He managed to start the engine, then with a clashing of gears, he got it into first gear and pulled the big rig out of the parking lot and onto the empty street. He drove a few blocks to a major home improvement center, while keeping an eye out for marauders and trying to learn the trick of shifting hears. He wondered how long the transmission would hold up as a result of the way he was abusing it.

It took him several tries to back the trailer up squarely to the loading dock at the back of the store. He entered the building through loading dock doors that had been left wide open, and found a propane powered fork lift. It was considerably easier to operate than the eighteen wheeler. The operating instructions were printed in bold black letters on its bright yellow dash board, and were pretty straightforward.

He was able to use the machine to load components for a pre-fabricated two-car garage that were strapped together on several different pallets. It was his hope that he would find an old road leading to some isolated forest grove where he might erect the structure and abandon the truck. In fact, it occurred to him that he might be able to live in the trailer itself.

Everything didn't go as smoothly as he'd have liked. At one point, he improperly balanced a load on the forks, and when he accidentally put the machine in reverse, he dumped several porcelain bath fixtures on the ground. He had to back away to avoid running over the shards. Later on, he punched a hole through the side of his trailer while trying to maneuver a stack of framing timbers.

He loaded a long list of items that included fiberglass insulation, dry wall and plywood sheeting, and flooring materials, plus plumbing and electrical supplies that he would need to convert the garage to a small cottage. *Why not?* he reasoned. *I have plenty of room on the trailer.*

Rummaging through the hardware department, he took two small electrical generators and a dozen gas cans. He took two of every tool he selected so that, if necessary, he could cannibalize one in order to keep the other going.

He found a carpenter's nail gun that intrigued him because it required neither electricity, air tank, nor hoses. It simply employed a small cylinder of gas and a battery to drive large nails into framing lumber.

A small high efficiency wood-burning stove with a catalytic converter joined the pile of materials. And he couldn't resist taking several solar panels that would convert sunlight to electricity, along with the connecting devices and a number of batteries to store the electricity.

CC found that making selections was very fatiguing. Each choice could ultimately extend or shorten his life. It was as though he'd been through this process before, and he wondered whether he had given thought to the issue of survival in the past. This question hovered in the background as he worked.

He had stacked the tools and materials on the floor just inside the warehouse so that he could estimate the size and mix of his load before putting anything on board. He sometimes discarded an item whose selection he had already painfully pondered. He would load a skid with the selected cartons, raise it to the back of the trailer, then arrange things by hand in order to pack them as compactly as possible.

Although he'd backed his trailer up to a loading dock at the back of the building, he couldn't shake the concern of being discovered by marauders, a fear that haunted him during the remainder of his time in Deep River Junction.

One item he treasured was a highly efficient low-pressure water purification system. He packed two of them, plus enough replacement filters to last for several years. To these were added a variety of plumbing materials, including copper and plastic tubing, fittings, solders, glues, and tools. Electrical supplies were treated in the same manner, with everything from a complete entry system, cable, boxes, fixtures, and even light bulbs, carefully packed and loaded. Roof shingles, paint, and a variety of other items, joined the growing load. His plans for a small home included every eventuality from primitive wood heat and tallow lighting to high-tech utilities, all depending upon the resources available.

He was meticulous about checking off each item on the detailed lists he had prepared, realizing that the lack of a single small item, such as solder flux, might make it impossible to complete a major job. He had a hazy memory of Saturday projects where he'd had to return to the hardware store several times before he got the right part to complete his task. There wouldn't be a hardware store around the corner if he were blessed to find a place to settle. There wouldn't be any stores at all!

Although he still experienced a sense of guilt that he was stealing, he didn't have to lay out cash for anything because there was no hint of ownership remaining. He nevertheless did a very strange thing. Taking a sheet of white cardboard and a felt marker, he wrote the name and address of the store, added "IOU $25,000," and signed it with the only name he knew, "CC." Then he tore it in half and dropped it on the floor. *Whether this comes under laws of abandonment and salvage,* he thought, *it's extremely unlikely that anyone will be alive to make a claim.* He thought of his own chances of survival and amended his thought. *It's unlikely that I will live to pay such a claim.*

He understood that the two matching generators he had loaded could only be run a few hours at a time, that they would quickly wear out, and would be useless when he ran out of gas and oil. When he weighed the advantages they offered in assembling the pre-fab building, however, their value far outweighed any space considerations. That decision necessitated his selecting a number of power tools. Whenever he selected an item like a drill or a power saw, he picked up two of each. Repairs and replacement parts were of vital importance. Redundancy was a major concern.

He realized that it would overload the truck to include two cubes of concrete blocks, but he did load a dozen bags each of mortar and portland cement so that he could use native stone if he needed to lay up footings or a chimney. And rather than clay tiles, he located sections of light-weight insulated metal stack that would make chimney construction quick and safe. Taking advantage of the weight saved, he loaded a refrigerator, electric range, microwave, and dishwasher, plus a washer and dryer, and assorted small appliances.

Where he would get the electrical power to operate them on a continuing basis eluded him. As he reflected on his choices, he realized that the decision to take these items was more a matter of denial—of clinging to the past in what was almost certainly false hope—rather than selecting wisely. He wasn't completely foolish, however.

He added an old-fashioned, cast-iron, wood-burning, kitchen stove. It would serve for both cooking and heating, but was also equipped with a boiler that would produce hot water for dish washing and bathing. The stove came unassembled, and weighed nearly 200 pounds. CC noted that he still had nearly half the cargo space available, and again feeling sheepish, he loaded a two-person whirlpool hot tub, laying it on edge against one wall of the trailer.

He spent very little time in the paint department, concentrating on flat enamels in tans, browns grays, blacks, and assorted greens. Before he left town, he planned to paint the truck and trailer. From now on, his favorite colors would be those that would camouflage his home and help him hide from the world.

Having spent nearly the entire day loading these items, he was exhausted, and decided to return to the hospital to pick up the medical supplies, bedding, and canned goods he'd left by the outside basement doors. He'd also gathered a quantity of surgical equipment and supplies, as well as antibiotics and painkillers that he'd discovered in the hospital store rooms and pharmacy. He would stack the more fragile of these items on the passenger side of the truck cab itself.

He understood that he would not be able to do much for

himself if he were seriously wounded or ill, but he harbored a hope that at some time in the future one or two other responsible individuals might join him. He realized that he was actually in greater danger from accidents or interlopers because, if he lived in isolation, the risk of communicable infection was nil.

He worked into the evening loading items at the hospital. Then, after grabbing some supper, he returned to the X-ray room to spend what was, he hoped, his last night in the hospital. In the morning he prepared a breakfast of bacon, eggs, hash browns, toast, coffee and orange juice, and savored every bite, knowing that it might be the last good breakfast he'd ever eat. *I will miss the fruit and vegetables,* he thought, *but I have no way to keep those frozen foods cold.*

He'd saved the last third of the trailer's floor space for the most vital items, food and water. And while he discovered over fifty cases of canned goods in the hospital, they were mostly large #10 cans. Once opened, unless refrigerated, they would spoil before he could consume their contents. So using the notes he'd made a week before, he located a wholesale food warehouse.

A very small sign out front contained only the name, "Lender Brothers," with no hint of the nature of the business. This suggested the reason that no one else had pillaged the place. He sorted through the warehouse, looking for foods in smaller containers with long shelf lives, but particularly for foods that he both liked and were nutritive.

He was very happy to discover a large stock of dry-frozen camping and hiking meals, and added them to the hundred odd cases of canned and packaged goods that he ultimately loaded onto the truck. He estimated that he had a three-year supply of food for four or more people. After loading the food, he added a wide variety of sundries, like dental floss, toothbrushes, and toilet tissue, realizing that he might never have access to anything like them again. Cases of paper plates and what would become irreplaceable cleaning products were carefully stacked in the trailer. Although he formerly favored "green" products, as a practical matter, any concern with saving the earth was far diminished.

He realized that potable water would be in short supply, and it might be some time before he could locate an isolated piece of land where he could establish a home and secure a good supply. So he loaded a pallet of bottled drinking water.

At a quality furniture store he picked up two twin beds, a dinette set with four chairs, a small desk and chair, a love seat, easy chair, and table, and a couple of lamps. CC picked the more compact pieces to save space. *Am I being overoptimistic in getting all this furniture,* he wondered, *or exercising some much-needed faith.*

Before he'd left the building supply, he'd loaded their forklift on the back of his tractor-trailer, and it proved very useful when he got to the wholesale food supplier. After he'd stacked boxes containing furniture on the truck, there was barely room to get it back aboard, but he had a feeling it might come in handy when unloading. There was still the matter of gathering a quantity of clothing, weapons, and ammunition for hunting and self-defense.

Those items were discovered at a sporting goods store. In addition to picking up sets of matching shotguns, rifles, and handguns, he loaded a large amount of ammunition and maintenance supplies. Then he added two compound bows and two cross bows along with arrows and bolts for all. He also picked up two sets each of cross-country skis, snowshoes, a light weight two-person kayak, assorted hunting knives, two all-terrain bicycles, and one electric bike. With these items, the truck was pretty much packed, and he suspected overweight. He had only about forty-square feet of unused floor area left of the original four hundred.

Again, he misjudged the time required, and found himself working into the late afternoon, so it was necessary to return to the hospital for the night. He was grateful for the things he had loaded, but was also aware that he would be foolish to place his trust in possessions.

My trust is in the Lord, he thought with sudden conviction. Yet, he felt that his faith was limited, and he was continually nagged by the concern that he might overlook something important. As a result, he frequently prayed for guidance.

Driving the big truck was a challenge, particularly now that he had such a heavy load. He was beginning to learn to shift the gears, but remained concerned that he'd rip out the transmission or use up the limited fuel before he located a remote place where he could build his hideaway.

Pulling back into the hospital service area, the thought came to him that he'd failed to pack a potato peeler, and he again wondered what other mundane but important items he might have overlooked. At least, he thought, he could take care of that omission while he was preparing what he was now sure was his final dinner at the hospital.

Like a kid waiting for Santa Claus, but without the legendary visions of sugar plums dancing through his head, it took him a long time to fall asleep that night. *The truth is,* he realized, *I'm afraid to take to the road and leave the illusion of security I enjoy here.* He lay awake for hours, checking things off his mental list, and it was about one in the morning before he finally thought of praying. He was so ashamed of this omission that he wound up spending twenty minutes apologizing to the Lord, and offering thanks, and didn't think to make a single petition. When he finally fell into a restless sleep, he tossed and turned a good deal. When morning arrived, he simply rolled back over and slept for another hour.

He felt exhausted when he awoke, and forced himself to bathe and shave before breakfast, knowing that he might never have the opportunity for another hot shower or a cooked meal. Then, more from fear of commitment than out of need, he wandered through the hospital's basement rooms, looking one more time to see whether he'd forgotten anything of value. He picked up a carton containing a new laptop computer, stacking it on the passenger seat.

He almost talked himself into waiting another day, but finally climbed up into the big rig and set out for the unknown. He was driving around the edge of town, looking for Route 19, when he spotted a book store. He left the truck in the middle of the village street, and entered the store. He spent over an hour selecting books, stacking them on a counter, then going through his selections a second time, arguing with himself that he could always return to the hospital for another night if he ran too late in the day.

Ultimately he loaded a dozen cases of books into the space remaining in the back of the trailer. They were on subjects as practical as camping, first-aid, surgery, homesteading, hunting, agriculture and animal husbandry, and building construction, and as seemingly impractical as art, history, and theology. When all was loaded, he made his way back to the religion section and put together an additional carton containing several versions of the Bible, a Strong's Concordance, several commentaries, and a few well-respected devotionals. He didn't bother with what he considered the popcorn and cotton candy devotionals written by prosperity-preaching demagogues. From his point of view, they had failed Christianity and America.

Escape from Boston

En route Boston to Vermont
May 7th, 7:30 a.m.

Elizabeth's post-nuclear experience below ground went from thirty minutes of terror to two weeks of tedium. At the end of that time she left her basement shelter, and made her way up the long flights of stairs to the underground garage which was located immediately below the museum's main floor.

Her 4X4 was still parked on the lower level of the museum garage, and she felt a great sense of relief when it started immediately. She exhausted herself making numerous trips up and down the five flights of stairs from the vault below to the parking garage, carrying the unspoiled food and other items she had packaged during what seemed her interminable wait. She also brought along a few other items she'd carefully packaged during her fourteen-day ordeal. By the time she'd carefully loaded the SUV, it was evening. She'd been hearing distant gunshots and, being afraid to venture out into the city after dark, she elected to lock her doors and sleep on the front seat of her vehicle.

Apart from the food from the caterer, which she'd long since either consumed or discarded, she'd found caches of canned goods and other treats left by employees who used the kitchen for their lunches, everything from packages of mac and cheese to canned chili. Although these didn't amount to much, they were decidedly better than nothing. She loaded all the clothing, including a change of both work and dress clothes that she'd kept in her locked office on the museum's first floor.

Whatever damage had been done to the rest of the city, it didn't seem too bad near the museum. Since she'd always liked to camp and hike, particularly along the back roads of New England, she looked forward to getting out of the city. She knew Boston well, and thought she could avoid major arteries while making her way northwest toward New Hampshire.

When morning came she was eager to get on her way, but forced herself to choke down a nutrition bar and a can of fruit juice. Then she headed through the suburbs toward 128 and the Turnpike. She knew that she'd been right about staying off the major highways when she got a glimpse of the Turnpike from a side street.

It was jammed with abandoned cars, and looked like an auto junk yard. And that's precisely what it had become, a miles long final cemetery for 21st Century motor vehicles. Many of them had obviously been wrecked in multiple car collisions, and there was total gridlock, but she saw no one moving about, nor did she stop to check.

Oddly enough, her GPS worked, and she was able to find alternate routes over lightly traveled streets. Sometimes she was forced to drive on the sidewalk to get around a traffic jam or to clear a blocked intersection, and sometimes she'd pick her way through an alley. Cars had simply been abandoned, and many roads were impassable. On two occasions, she had to back up and find another route. She heard occasional gunshots, and adjusted her route away from them. The four-wheel drive vehicle was phenomenal, and proved a life-saver when a gang of hoodlums on foot chased her, and she was forced to drive across a vacant lot and up and down the steep grassy slopes of a city park in order to evade them.

She crossed into New Hampshire, and found an abandoned gas station on a narrow country road. It was just a little mom and pop store, with clapboard siding, old cola signs, and two gas pumps out front. She stripped the shelves of canned goods, loading them into the back of her SUV, trusting they hadn't been contaminated by radiation. She'd heard on the radio that cans that were heavily radiated would themselves became radioactive. It would be suicide to handle them, let alone eat anything they contained. She still had room in the truck, so she loaded a couple of cases of engine oil. It occurred to her that some items would soon be more valuable than gold, and she might be able to barter the lubricants.

Without electricity, the gas pumps wouldn't operate, but she was able to siphon fuel from a couple of parked cars. With her tank full, she continued toward the northwest. The few refugees she passed along the road made her extremely nervous. After her experience at the museum, strangers represented a collective danger, so she raced away from them as she searched for a her own place of survival. She crossed New Hampshire, and headed into the mountains of central Vermont.

Crossing the Hudson

Lake Katrine, New York
May 7th, 8:30 a.m.

After two weeks in the mushroom caverns, Jonathan rode

his bike to the church. When he approached the front doors, he was driven back by the stench of decay. Violently ill and sick at heart, he started his father's pickup truck with the spare key he'd brought from home. Sitting there with the motor idling, he gazed at the old frame building, the paint pealing from the dry old clapboard siding. It looked so sad, and yet he'd spent so many wonderful hours within. *And now its my parents' final resting place,* he thought.

He had an idea, and on impulse he shut down the truck engine. He began wandering around the perimeter of the property looking for empty glass bottles among the weeds. He found four. Returning to the unpaved parking lot, he began trying car doors. When he found one that had been left unlocked, he raised the hood, leaned over the engine, and ripped out a long vacuum hose. He popped the gas tank cover, and using the hose, he siphoned gasoline into each of the four bottles. It was a certainty that its owner would have no further use for the gasoline or the vehicle.

There was an old rag in the bed of his father's pick up. He tore it into four pieces, and stuffed a strip tightly into the top of each of the bottles. Taking three of the gas filled bottles, he stood about five paces from the side of the building, and heaved each of them through a different window. Sadly, the sound of breaking glass did not rouse the inhabitants of the building

Tears streaming down his face, he now stood about ten paces from the side of the old frame building, and tipped the last of the bottles upside down to let the gasoline saturate the cloth. Taking care not to burn himself, and hoping the bottle wouldn't explode in his hands, he held it as far from his body as he could, and lit the rag. The flame rose a couple of feet, and in a panic, he almost dropped the bottle. Regaining control of himself, he launched it sidearm at one of the windows. He missed the window, but the bottle broke against the wall of the church, bursting into flame. Within seconds the flame spread over the dry old boards, and the heat became so intense that he had to back away.

He watched as the flames licked up the side of the building, rolling in yellow waves beneath the soffit, then eating their way into the attic. The fire spread quickly. With a whoosh, the gasoline inside the building caught, and flames shot out of all the windows. Within minutes, the entire building was involved.

Jonathan was driven back, shocked by the result of his actions. Then he smelled something strange, like meat broiling, and when he realized what it was, he fell to his knees and became ill. Lost in his own sickness and sorrow, it took him a moment to realize that he was in danger of being burned alive. He leapt to his feet and ran for his dad's truck. Turning onto the highway, he had one last glimpse of the building. It was engulfed in flames, even it's little steeple aglow. As he accelerated away, he thought it a fitting funeral pyre for God's people.

As he drove toward home, he didn't see a single car or pedestrian. In fact, with the exception of a few birds, he didn't see any animals either.

Arriving home, he began loading his father's old pickup with the same items the two of them would have taken on a hunting trip. After he'd ransacked the house for food and anything else he thought might be of value, he drove north on 9-W toward Albany.

He repeatedly asked himself why he had left home, and had deserted everything he considered familiar in order to head out into the unknown. He could think of only two reasons. First, he couldn't stand to stay at home knowing that his parent's remains were just a few miles away. Second, a radio commentator had announced that northern New England had received very little fallout. Whether that was an accurate report, he had no idea, but since the New England states had small populations, it seemed like a good place to head for.

As he drove north, he caught occasional glimpses of the Hudson River down across the fields on his right. He was just south of Catskill, the legendary home of Rip Van Winkle, and was passing a quarry on his left, when the engine began to sputter. Checking the gauge, he realized that he was out of gas. *Very smart,* he thought. *I siphoned gasoline to burn the church, and didn't think to fill the truck.* Before the engine quit, he turned right on Embought Road. Nursing the engine along, and praying under his breath, he coasted downhill between fields and woodlands toward the west shore of the Hudson.

Leaving the vehicle in a cul-de-sac at the end of the road, he wandered along the shoreline. He discovered an old row boat, with a set of splintered oars. It was hidden among a heavy growth of cattails near the trackbed of the old New York Central Westside. Making several round trips, he loaded the boat with his survival gear, hoping all the time that it wouldn't sink under him. Then, on that clear, still afternoon, he rowed slowly across the broad, island-spotted Hudson to a cove on the east bank where more railroad tracks hugged the shore line.

After spending the night in a copse of trees near the tracks, he made a pack of what he considered his most important possessions, and walked north on the roadbed until he noticed a building off to his right. This brought him to

Station Road, and a little later, to old Route 9-G, the Rhinebeck-Hudson Road.

Preppers Hideaway

Central Vermont
May 8th, 6:10 p.m.

For over a decade, they had enjoyed their snug little cabin, but finally came to agree that it would offer too little protection from fallout, and too little space for their growing families. So they had built this sophisticated shelter in a cleft in the side of the rock ledge that rose about fifty feet above their old log road.

A deep indentation in the escarpment had provided them sufficient depth and height to construct a two-story concrete block shelter, and, like engineers at a theme park, they had spent weeks troweling cement over wire mesh to convert what remained of the deep gash in the cliff face into a natural looking bulge.

Now the two men were looking out through a narrow irregular slit that, from the ground below, simply looked like a fault in the cliff wall.

"You've had the binoculars long enough, Michael. Let me take a look."

As he handed him the glasses, he commented, "It's a woman, John, and she's alone."

The woman had stopped her 4×4 on the far side of the stream that ran along the base of the cliff, and the second man adjusted the binoculars to get a clearer view. He was wearing khaki slacks and a white shirt, the words, "Deep

River Junction Fire Department" printed on the back, and just the word, "Chief" over the left breast.

"She's a looker," he remarked.

"Oh, really?" his wife laughed, moving up behind them.

"Oops," laughed the first man. "Now you're in for it."

"No need to warn him, sheriff," she laughed in turn. "I'm better at putting out fires than he is...at least the important ones."

They all laughed because her husband had won numerous awards for his heroism and skill in fighting fires and saving lives.

"Yeah, that's true," he agreed with his wife, not at all discomfited.

"What's she doing?" queried the woman.

"I'm guessing that she's just trying to find a place to hide."

John didn't need the binoculars to follow her movements into the trees. "Yeah, and it looks like she's found it," he responded.

"So the question is, what do we do about her."

"Well, we aren't inviting her up here," the woman intoned.

"Why not?" her sister-in-law laughed, entering the conversation. "Too much competition?"

"Well, that too," the first woman responded. "But, truth be told, we are pretty crowded, and we can only add so many people with the food available, so we'll have to be very careful about who we invite to join us."

"Right!" laughed the other woman. "I'm thinking in terms of a real hunk."

"Ah, come on girls! We're not that bad, are we?"

"All joking aside," the fire chief interrupted, "we've agreed that whoever we bring on board has to be a real contributor, preferably a trained soldier, but definitely a good woodsman."

Michael turned to them. "Yes. This is as serious a situation as I can imagine. There are probably thousands of decent people running around Vermont like this woman, but we can't help them all. We have to keep our eye on our ultimate goal, and that's to gather people with the skill and determination to restore our republic. And we need to remember that Jamie might still make it here."

"So," John interjected, "that brings us back to the question of what we do about her."

"I'd say nothing," was the reply. "Let her take what little food and whatever else we left in the cabin, and go her way. We can get along without it."

"Where is she now? Has she discovered the cabin?" asked one of the women.

"Not yet. But soon. She's wandering around the meadow as though looking for a place to camp."

"Let me see," his wife ordered, and he handed her the glasses.

"Well, I'll be! she intoned.

"What?"

"I think I know her," the woman muttered.

"Well, that puts a new light on things," the other man replied.

"No, no, I don't mean I actually know her." She hesitated. Where's that New York Sunday supplement I was looking at this morning?"

"On the table. Why?"

The woman handed the glasses back to Michael, and

crossed the big room that served as kitchen, dining room, living room, gym, and observation post.

"Here it is."

"What?"

"She looks just like the woman in this photograph."

They passed the page around, each one studying the photo.

"Yes, it sure looks like her. What about it?"

"She worked in an art museum in Boston."

"So?"

"Nothing, really. It says here that she was responsible for setting up a display of the "Declaration of Independence" that was supposed to open about the time the war started."

Michael had the duty, and was still posted at the observation window.

"She's found the cabin."

"Fine. Let her have it."

"Agreed. There's no advantage in becoming involved with her, and no justification for hindering her."

"Okay, it's a bit inconvenient, but we'll keep an eye on her, and when we need to go outside for exercise, we'll head over the crest to the valley east of us."

Vacant Cabin

Central Vermont
May 8th, 6:10 p.m.

Exhausted, and desperately in need of sleep, she discovered a narrow, rutted track, half-hidden by underbrush.

It was hardly wide enough to admit a vehicle, and once again her 4X4 justified its purchase. She drove as far up the overgrown lane as she could, then got out for a stretch and a little exploration.

That's when she discovered an old summer camp hidden in a dense stand of pines, overlooking a small lake. The place was idyllic, and judging from the weeds in the long driveway, no one seemed to have been there in some time. She'd found the front door key under a rock, and decided to hide out there for as long as it would take the world to settle back to normal.

The cabin was well-stocked with supplies, as though the owners regularly visited there. Perhaps, she thought, they had planned to come here in an emergency like this, but never made it. She was saddened by the thought, and found herself saying a brief prayer for their well-being. She locked her vehicle, returned to the cabin, and began setting up housekeeping.

Her spirits were lifted when she noticed several shelves stacked with good books. When she lifted a rug with the intention of taking it outside to shake it out, she discovered a trap door that hid a root cellar beneath the cottage. The cellar contained a large cache of canned goods, two gas lanterns and a supply of fuel. In the woodshed out back, there were six cans of gas, each containing five gallons. And there were several bottles of gasoline stabilizer. Under a bed, in a long narrow carton, she found an army surplus thirty-caliber carbine, along with an owner's manual, a cleaning kit, and three hundred rounds of ammunition. There was a canvas sling on the rifle, and fastened to the sling were two canvas pouches. These each contained two magazines for the weapon, and each magazine contained fifteen rounds.

After closing and locking the shutters on all the windows,

and dropping the heavy wooden bars into the slots on the inside of both the front and rear doors, she felt far more secure. Someone might break in, but it would be difficult, especially if she was firing the carbine at them.

After she'd eaten a can of spaghetti, she sat down by lantern light to read the owner's manual for the carbine. With some difficulty she followed the instructions to field strip and reassemble the weapon, carefully cleaning and oiling each piece.

On the second day, she'd backed her car behind a clump of brush, and filled the gas tank from the cans in the woodshed. The four remaining cans went into the back of the vehicle. She walked back down to the main road to look for anyone that might be in the area. Seeing no one, she took care to straighten the weeds that had been bent over by her vehicle's tires.

Elizabeth remained at the cabin for about six weeks. She started the car every week, and ran it for about five minutes to keep the battery charged. When she estimated that she had only enough food remaining to last a few weeks, she knew she would have to move on. Later, she would wish that she'd simply remained there and tried to locate food somewhere else in the area.

Her first night back on the road, she pulled in among some trees to get some sleep. The next morning, as she was preparing to move on, she was attacked.

Hate at First Sight

Looter's Campsite
South of Deep River Junction, Vermont
May 8th, 6:15 p.m.

Elizabeth lay on her back, her muscles cramping, her hands tied in front of her. The old tent in which she was being held stunk of alcohol and pot. The buttons of her shirt had been torn off, but so far she hadn't been sexually abused. She wondered how much more time she could possibly have, but she wasn't ready to give up.

She tugged at the tight bindings that held her wrists, even as she strained to listen for her captors' return. For the moment she could identify no alien sound coming from the campground. All of the looters had ridden their motorcycles down to their roadblock.

Then she heard someone approaching, and stopped tugging at the ropes, willing herself not to breathe. She stifled a scream of terror as she saw a knife blade plunge down through the canvas just above her head, then watched as the blade was dragged across the side of the tent. It couldn't be one of her captors, she reasoned. They would simply have come in through the flap at the front.

The knife blade turned, and was dragged in an L across the canvas, causing the loose triangle to drop down and drag across her face, obscuring her view. Twisting her head, she looked up through the opening and saw a face, a very handsome face.

She was about to scream, but the man held his finger over his lips, signaling silence. She stifled the confusion of questions that rose to mind, and instead found herself uttering something completely irrelevant.

"You're Matthew Sennett!"

He nodded, but simply said, "And I've seen your picture in the paper too, and you're even more beautiful than your photos." He reached down with the knife, and she raised her bound hands to protect herself, but he simply grasped them in one huge hand, and used the razor-sharp knife to cut her free.

Seeing his eyes move down her body, she reached down and pulled the torn front of her shirt together.

Braced for something unpleasant, his next words surprised her. "Did they hurt you?"

At a loss for words, she just shook her head quickly from side to side.

When she looked back at him, he was studying her eyes. He whispered, "We've got to hurry!"

"I'm not going anywhere with you," she hissed.

"I'm helping you escape."

"I don't need your help."

"Well, you certainly did a moment ago."

"Well, I don't need it anymore."

My God, he has a nice smile. But I've read too much about him. It would be like jumping out of the frying pan and leaping into the fire.

He started to say, "Beggars can't be choosers," but in the middle of the sentence, there was the sound of a motorcycle coasting to a stop near the tent. She rose to her knees, her head rising through the hole in the canvas that her rescuer or assailant, she couldn't decide which, had just cut. Seeing a clean-cut biker who had not been among her captors, she stood in the opening, stepped out of the tent, and began running toward him, crying for help. At the same time, she heard the report of a rifle from down near the roadblock, and a small branch was snapped off a tree above her head.

Sennett saw the man on the bike, and shouted to her, "Don't, you'll be safer with me." As he reached for her, she caught up a piece of firewood laying by her feet, spun, and struck him across the side of the head, knocking him to the ground. She ran toward the bike, then stopped in indecision.

"Well, are you coming or not?" the cyclist demanded. When she remained motionless, he spun the wheels and headed out between two trees.

"Please," she shouted, "take me with you." He turned the bike, pine needles spraying out behind him, as he wheeled around and slid to a stop by her.

"Well?" he demanded.

"Wait a second," she hollered. Skirting the place where the man who had cut her loose was trying to push himself up from the ground, she reached into the tent and lifted out a large black portfolio. While the guy on the bike revved the engine, she threw her leg over the back of the seat, wrapped her arms around the portfolio, and somehow grasped the sides of his leather jacket. He let out the clutch and began racing away.

Several rifles were firing up the hill from the roadblock when the big man finally pulled himself to his feet and staggered off into the thick woods in pursuit of the pair on the motorcycle.

Out of Fuel

State Highway 19
Central Vermont
May 9th, 7:18 p.m.

He had been eyeing the fuel gauge with increasing concern, and shifted down through the gears as the eighteen-wheeler slowed on the upgrade. Now his unease turned to resolve, and he determined to shut the big rig down after he crossed over the crown of the hill.

He had to give himself time to consider his next move, but his options were evaporating with every ounce of diesel fuel consumed. Fuel had become a precious and vanishing commodity, and he hadn't been able to add anything to the small amount he had at the beginning of the trip. Even if he had been able to locate a service station with a diesel pump, with the power off, it would have been nearly impossible to find the means to pump it out of its underground storage tank.

He was angry at himself for loading the utility generators so far forward in the trailer, for he might have used one of them to power a diesel pump, if he'd found one. It was a moot point. He had passed only one gas station since leaving the hospital, and it had been gutted by fire.

CC realized that he must get the rig off the road and under cover, or he would lose his hard-earned cargo to the first gang of marauders that happened along. He knew that he must somehow locate an untraveled lane wide enough to handle his heavy sixty-five-foot rig. He doubted that he had sufficient fuel remaining to travel more than ten or fifteen miles, and he knew that he had little hope of finding such an untraveled lane on the side of this rugged New England mountain. Looking downhill in front of him, the stone wall on his right served as a guard rail above the sheer cliff that shadowed the valley far below. On his left was an escarpment that rose almost vertically for nearly two hundred feet above the road.

His truck had one of the finest audio systems he'd ever seen, and he reasoned that, at this elevation, he might pick up a signal. He punched the search button on the AM band. The static was interrupted by a truculent voice. An obviously non-professional announcer was stumbling over the reading of a statement demanding that all listeners move to major designated population centers or find themselves in violation of martial law. The espoused purpose was to help provide for the welfare of citizens by conducting a census.

The speaker stammered over the words as he declared that the headcount would "...permit the interim government to more effectively guide the economy, disseminate information, and redistribute available resources."

Ah, thought CC. *More "redistribution" of wealth.*

The announcer continued, "Anyone found outside these designated centers after May 10th without a government permit will be assumed to be a looter. Looters," he declared, "will be shot on sight." He continued, "The leaders of the interim government understand the problems faced by refugees, and will, for the time being, only fire on those who attempt to flee. If an individual has in his possession any item for which he cannot produce an original receipt, that item will be considered loot."

CC ground his teeth in anger. I wonder how many people have a receipts for the clothes they are wearing, much less the can of beans they might have brought from home.

The announcer went remorselessly on. "All loot will be

confiscated and the looter held for imprisonment or execution subject to an administrative hearing."

Well, that answers that, he thought. *If you fail to enter their detention centers, you're subject to being shot. If you're apprehended, you'd better have receipts for everything in your possession, or be standing there naked. On the other hand, according to what I've heard from the ham broadcasters, these guys are apt to strip everyone, especially the women.*

The announcer added, "To protect your safety, there is an absolute ban on firearms. Anyone found possessing a firearm of any kind, or ammunition for a firearm, or any explosive device, or any materials with which an explosive device might be made, will be summarily executed."

Well, CC thought, *explosive materials could theoretically include almost any petroleum derivative, such as gasoline or oil, and even items one might find in the potting shed, such as fertilizer.* He recalled how the Oklahoma City bombing was the result of combining fertilizer with diesel fuel oil in the back of a rental truck.

Then, of course, there's the container in which an explosive might be housed, such as a child's backpack, or the flashlight batteries that might be used to detonate it. The list goes on and on. So the "authorities" can pretty much find a reason to charge almost anyone with bomb-building and terrorism.

The announcer concluded with the promise that listeners would be well provided for once they reached the designated centers.

We're being forced to travel to the promised land, with all the biblical promises of milk and honey. Unfortunately, he mused, *it sounds more like it is Adolf Hitler, and not God, who is making the promises.*

CC had already heard a report that one group was making a concerted effort to steal the meager possessions of refugees like himself, and then turn the people into slaves in some sort of twentieth-century feudal system. The thought found him unconsciously patting his handgun. Its presence gave him a greater sense of security than any of the *new order's* deceitful promises.

His eyes were again drawn to the dash board. The little fuel pump icon was now illuminated. CC was down to his last gallon or two of diesel fuel.

"Well," he said aloud, as he stepped back down from the cab, "when all else fails, try prayer," and he knelt on the grass beside the wall and bowed his head.

Police Headquarters

Rutland, VT
May 9th, 7:30 p.m.

Rachel had blundered onto the roadblock because she'd been dividing her attention between the twilit road ahead and her efforts to search the woods on either side for a turn off where she might hide for the night.

The presence of a man in police uniform had initially deceived her and put her somewhat at ease, but subsequent events revealed how foolish she had been in failing to attempt to flee.

The fact that he was a real cop did nothing to keep the piratical group at the road block from rifling her truck and seizing all her possessions for themselves, although she suspected that he had saved her from a far worse fate, for the so-called soldiers manning the roadblock were made up of the dregs of society. It was something of a relief when the officer handcuffed her and drove her to the local police headquarters where the worst that happened was that she received a number of lustful looks.

She was led into a candle lit room, seated at a table, the handcuffs removed, and then left alone. It occurred to her that this was like some bad apocalyptic TV police drama, but since it was happening to her, it was nothing to laugh about. She assumed that she was being observed through the large mirror that covered much of one wall, so she made it a point to remain as still as possible.

After about an hour, an interrogator came in accompanied by a middle-aged couple. They were introduced as the Burtons, and she was told that, depending on her answers, she might be released into their custody as an indentured servant. "Otherwise," the officer intoned, "your future might not be so pleasant." Based on the looks she'd received from the men at the roadblock, as well as those who'd ogled her while entering police headquarters, she had a pretty good idea of what that future might consist.

The officer set a glass of water in front of her, told her she'd better tell her story, and leaned back in his chair, his arms crossed behind his head.

In spite of a throat made dry from anxiety, Rachel interrupted her story only once to take a sip of the water. The Burtons listened intently, from time to time exchanging cryptic looks, and she had no idea whether they were impressed with her candor or believed her story. She would have been surprised to learn that they considered her incredibly naïve, and that they felt they could use her innocence to their advantage.

Rachel was straightforward in giving an account of her survival. She didn't mention that she was in the caverns for a wedding, nor did she provide any unsolicited information concerning her past. When she finished her tale, she simply said, “Just outside Rutland I was picked up by the Home Guard. You know the rest.”

The policeman turned to the Burtons. “Well, you heard her,” he said. “She seems innocent enough to me, if maybe a little simple. If you want her, she'll go to work for you. If not, we'll put her in a special home where she will entertain troops. It's up to you.”

The woman sucked on a tooth for a moment, then asked a question.

“Let me get this straight. If we don't think she's working hard enough, we can hold the threat of her being put in that special home over her head. Is that right?”

The cop frowned, obviously uncomfortable with the question. Then he nodded his head, speaking quietly. “That's it,” he agreed.

“Okay. We'll take her off your hands,” she stated peremptorily, as though she were doing them both a favor.

The Cleft in a Rock

State Highway 19
Central Vermont
May 9th, 7:32 p.m.

He had been heading north when he finally pulled the truck to a stop just over the crest of the mountain highway. He turned the selector from AM to the police scanner setting, then turned the truck's wheels sharply left so that, if the breaks failed, it would roll across the shoulder and into the trees beneath the towering cliff. He then pulled an aluminum wheel chock from the floor of the cab, jumped to the ground, and rammed it in front of one of the tires.

Taking a moment to stretch his legs, he looked over the rig. A few gallons of paint and a long-handled roller had transformed the cab and trailer into a camouflaged mess of tan, green and black smears. Before he'd left the hospital, he'd walked down the length of the trailer roof, overlapping blotches of the assorted colors. Then he'd worked from the top down each side. It wasn't pretty, but parked where it was next to the trees below the escarpment, it was far less visible.

He mentally dismissed the condition of the rig, knowing that for better or worse it would serve him for only a few more miles. Returning his attention to his plight, he made his way over to the rock retaining wall that ran along the east side of the highway. The dizzying elevation offered a spectacular view of the valley below. It was obvious that deliverance did not lay in that direction. The setting sun was casting a final golden glow across the far side of the valley, and it was clear that there was no traffic on the narrow road that ran down its far side. At this time of year, he knew that the sun would be completely down by 8 pm, so he had only about thirty minutes until nightfall.

Just as he began to relax, his attention was caught by a small, low-flying plane on the far side of the valley. The electronic scanner was homing on the plane's radio, and just as CC spotted it, his truck's speaker squawked with some unintelligible static. He realized with a sense of panic that the pilot was looking for him, or rather, he was looking for people like him who hadn't moved to one of those designated centers. CC had seen the burned and gutted remains of many cars and trucks during the course of his short journey, and he knew that it was only a matter of time before the pilot looked up from the valley floor and spotted his tractor-trailer parked on the mountain road.

Apart from his amateurish camouflage job, his one advantage lay in the fact that his truck sat in the shadow of the cliffs, while the setting sun was probably glaring over the mountaintop into the pilot's eyes.

Nonetheless, the day suddenly seemed cold and dark. He'd been regularly monitoring the ham operators on citizen-band radio, and he'd gotten the impression that multitudes were starving while a few privileged were living in luxury in an area relatively untouched by nuclear fallout. This so-called "safe area" was supposedly comprised of parts of northeastern New York, northern Massachusetts, and all of Vermont, New Hampshire, and Maine.

With the precious load he was hauling, he held no illusions about the kind of treatment he could expect if captured. Ham radio operators had been filling the airwaves with reports about the avaricious assortment of thieves and ne'er-do-wells they laughingly called "The New Order." He'd even heard a report that a Chinese infantry battalion had set up headquarters in Burlington, and that they were in turn fighting several hundred Islamic fundamentalists who were also attempting to gain control of what had been New England. *Well, at least the bad guys are fighting with one another,* he thought. *Maybe they'll kill one another off and save us survivors the trouble.*

CC had stopped his truck on the left side of the road, as close to the trees that grew beneath the cliff as he could get, so that it would be more difficult to spot. The highway curved sharply here, and seemed to hang on the edge of the cliff. Although he had passed the crest of the hill, and was parked well downhill, the top of the escarpment rose far above him. To his right, on the east side of the narrow highway, there was a nearly vertical drop of about two-hundred feet to the valley below. On his left, to the west, there was an equally impossible climb.

In order to carve this road into the side of the near vertical slope, it was obvious that the drillers had driven their bits deep into the native rock, and the powder men had blasted huge quantities of stone down the mountain side, creating a deep notch in the cliff face to serve as the roadbed. Here and there, massive spurs of natural rock extended out five and ten yards on the valley side of the road. These massive shelves were below the highway, and appeared as though they were glued to the mountainside and suspended above the valley.

CC walked across the road and leaned his elbows on the stone retaining wall, and stared out across the valley. It was a beautiful evening, sunny and dry. He was looking at, but not really seeing, the distant airplane. He reached for the radiation detection badge pinned to his shirt, and tipped it up so that he could examine the reading. It hadn't changed. The level was very low. He should have felt good about that, but an enemy who presumably didn't even know he existed was flying down the valley toward him, little more than two miles away.

Gradually he became aware that the sound he took for the distant aircraft engine was really the noise of falling water, it's dull roar finally piercing his baneful musings. Curiosity got the best of him. He pushed himself up so that his head hung over the top of the wall, and stared down the cliff.

About thirty feet beneath him, the end of an enormous steel culvert pipe protruded from under the highway. Water spewed out of the pipe onto a broad rock ledge, then swept between the broken stone abutments of a bridge long since removed, swirled about the moss-covered surface, swelled behind a natural dam of large boulders, and finally arced over the precipice to cascade to the valley below.

Since there was not a wide enough shoulder on either side of the highway to permit parking, and signs along both sides of the road forbade stopping, the casual passerby would never notice the madly rushing stream that the engineers had hidden so well. The massive stone wall that kept traffic from careening over the edge of the cliff also effectively hid any view of the outfall below. And on the mountain side, a heavy growth of mature pines and assorted scrub blocked a view of the uphill end of the culvert pipe and the location of the stream that fed into it.

He wondered at the phenomenon of a large stream flowing out of the side of a mountain. Curiosity dictated that he take a moment to search for the source, so he slid back off the wall and turned toward the mountain, searching for the stream that must flow beneath the cliff along the opposite side of the road before being swallowed by the culvert to cross beneath the highway. Seeing no trace of a stream, he crossed the highway to gain a better look.

The cliff curved back away from the highway at this point, leaving a crescent-shaped strip of land between itself and the road. Within that crescent, at the base of the cliff, grew a thick stand of evergreens. Along the edge of the highway itself, the engineers had cut a swale to carry runoff down the mountain. Apart from that, he could see no evidence of a stream on the other side of the road. The mystery of the underground river bemused him, so he crossed back to the valley side.

Leaning back against the stone retaining wall, he scanned the cliff face, searching for any telltale indication of the stream's source. He hoped to spot a cleft or a cave from which the stream must flow. Perhaps he might find space to secrete some of his precious cargo before abandoning the truck further down the highway. He groaned with disappointment when he realized that no such opening was discernible in the gathering gloom beneath the cliff.

He again looked up to study the cliff face. Something caught the light from the setting sun as it slipped into view near the top of the cliff. For an instant, as his tired eyes tried to make the adjustment from twilight to the glare of evening sky above, he imagined it to be the searching plane, but to his great relief, he realized that it was a hawk, flying across the face of the cliff. A magnificent bird, it appeared black against the corduroy gray of the escarpment.

It beat rapidly upward and would have been lost to sight were it not for the last glow of sunset painting the sky. The hawk circled for a moment or two, then dove with tremendous speed toward the edge of the highway, just down the hill from where he was standing. Scarcely slowing, the bird caught a rabbit in its dagger-like talons, swooped back up above the roadway, and without climbing appreciably, shot back toward the cliff. CC had expected it to sit back on its tail feathers to brake its speed, then settle into some nesting place on the cliff face. He was surprised when the predator appeared to fly headlong at the impenetrable rock wall, its prey in its claws, and then disappeared above the tree tops into a shadow in the rocks.

He shook his head in puzzlement. He realized that there

had to be a cleft in the rock, some sort of an opening in the cliff face. An inexplicable feeling of assurance flowed over him. This might be the miracle he'd been praying for. It had to be! The conduit beneath his feet must receive its flow from somewhere up a narrow ravine that ran through the mountain. How else could it deliver that huge quantity of water below the highway's brink?

He sprinted for the trees at the base of the cliff. In the twilight he could detect a narrow shadow that started high up the cliff face, then folded in upon itself, and darkened as it fell nearly vertically to the tree tops. The casual observer would overlook this fault in the cliff face because it was hidden by the tall row of pines that grew along its base. From a speeding automobile, few would even imagine the existence of such an opening. Actually the typical traveler would probably be looking out across the picturesque valley rather than gazing into the trees at the foot of the escarpment.

CC ran toward the point beneath which the hawk had disappeared, counting on finding some kind of opening in the rock behind the screen of trees, and praying that the solution to this mystery might also provide the solution to his survival.

He pushed through the low-hanging boughs, the scratches on his arms unnoticed as his eyes probed the gloom. He unexpectedly found himself in a leafy corridor, a narrow defile leading back into the mountain. It must have been cut through the rock by countless ages of flowing water, but still he saw no stream.

He walked slowly back up this ravine, astonished at the mystery and beauty of the place. It seemed clear now that the rows of trees that bordered the highway had been carefully spaced by the highway's builders, but behind those trees, funneling up into the heart of the mountain, and shaded by its mass, was a narrow defile, almost choked by huge ancient oaks. It was rocky, overgrown, and rugged, but the congestion proved an illusion, for those giant hardwoods were also well spaced, their huge limbs spreading out to intertwine with one another, effectively hiding the ground below from anyone who might fly above them.

He stopped in mid-stride, almost tripping himself, amazement turning to delight. Darkness surrounded him, but ahead of him the sunlight spilled through an opening in the rocks, turning the trees into a mass of translucent greens and blues. And down the center of the narrow ravine there were only fallen leaves and tender saplings.

Now that he had penetrated the cliff that shaded the highway, the setting sun beckoned him on. Was it welcoming him to a new hope, or enticing him to a final disappointment?

End of "War's Desolation"

A Preview of the next Book in the
***The Chronicles of CC*,**
"The Heav'n Rescued Land"

He stopped in mid-stride, almost tripping over his own feet, his amazement turning to delight. Darkness surrounded CC, but ahead of him the sunlight spilled through an opening in the rocks, turning the trees into a mass of translucent greens, golds and blues. And down the center of the narrow ravine there were only fallen leaves and tender saplings.

Now that he had penetrated the cliff that shaded the highway, the setting sun beckoned him on. Was it welcoming him to a new hope, or enticing him to disappointment? A few hundred paces further along, he heard the sound of flowing water. It was off to the left edge of the widening defile. He moved on, and discovered a small lake where water from further up the valley was gathered before being gulped down by a huge culvert pipe. He'd found the source of the stream that flowed beneath the highway.

CC kicked at the thick layer of composting leaves beneath his feet and, to his delight, discovered that they hid the remains of a crumbling macadam road. The pungent odor of rotting vegetation evoked thoughts of hiking and camping, and promised the isolated sort of environment which he had been seeking. He wasn't going to take time to ponder why this abandoned road existed. His curiosity, and maybe something more, had brought him a great opportunity. Now he needed to capitalize on potential. If it was not already too late, he had to get his tractor-trailer into this narrow canyon before the pilot of that meandering plane spotted the rig.

As he ran back out of the trees that bordered the road, he threw a glance in the direction in which he'd last seen the light aircraft, but it was no longer in view. Knowing that time was against him, he took a quick look to gauge the distance between the larger of the trees, and measured with his eyes the likelihood of driving the rig between them. With his inexperience, it seemed a slight chance, but he also knew he would never find a better hideaway. It was his intent to get off the highway and move the truck as far as possible up this narrow canyon. There, he suspected, it would remain forever. Whether he could succeed or not, his circumstances compelled him to make the attempt. In the gathering darkness, he quickly surveyed the path he would take.

He wondered briefly what natural forces had created this improbable gap in the mountain wall, but could not afford the luxury of time to dwell on the question. A geologist might have told him that enormous forces of fire and pressure from within the earth's core had twisted the amorphous mass near the surface, resulting in a radical dip in the mountains, an anticline, and that the bottom of that cleft had formed a box canyon through which a mountain stream tumbled. He might have argued that the stream took thousands of years to cut its way down through the rock, reshaping the valley until, in the recent past, the engineers had redirected its path. And it therefore now churned its way through the culvert pipe that was buried beneath the highway, finally leaping free to crash from ledge to ledge down the mountain's steep side to the valley below.

Running back toward the truck, he caught a glimpse of the plane returning to the crossroads far up the valley. His chest was heaving now, the result of running while wearing a lead X-ray apron and breathing through a nuisance dust mask. Realizing that he could not save the truck while worrying about the radiation count, he slipped out of the vest, let it drop beneath the trees, and again took off running toward the truck.

As CC reached the edge of the road, he took note of the broad shallow ditch that the highway's builders had dug parallel to the pavement to carry off rainwater. This swale had been cut across the end of the hidden lane he needed to enter. It didn't simply disguise the old log road, it effectively severed the end of it. He was doubtful that he could drive the overloaded rig across, but he had no choice but to try.

He had shut the engine down to conserve fuel. Now, as he pulled himself up into the cab, he thought of the maddening seconds he might have to wait to preheat the big diesel. He cranked up the compressed air and hit the starter. It exploded into operation, catching on the first try. Breathing a prayer of thanks, he slammed it into reverse and backed up so violently that he almost jackknifed the trailer into the stone retaining wall.

Pulling the wheel around hand-over-hand, he cut the tractor across the uphill lane, gunning the engine hard as the cab approached the ditch at nearly a ninety-degree angle. The engine seemed to fade a little as it lost torque, but then began to roar again, and he felt power surging to the drive axles. It careened down into the swale and the front wheels began to plow the thin layer of muck at the bottom. The rig slowed frighteningly as the wheels dug in, but the weight of the trailer saved him. Just as he thought the tractor would bog down and stop, the momentum of that massive load pushed the back of the cab down and forward on bouncing wheels, driving the front wheels of the cab up and out of the ditch onto firmer ground.

Uncertain what to do, he kept the pedal on the floor, hoping to avoid fish-tailing. Time seemed to stand still as the tractor's rear wheels spun in the mud, then slowly began to climb out of the swale. He again thought he was defeated when the cab began to slide sideways and the rig began to jackknife. If it slid too far, he'd smash the side of the trailer into the trees or hang up in the ditch. It was a close thing, but the tractor's eight drive wheels with their brand-new tires suddenly caught, and the load began to creep forward again. In their turn, the eight wheels supporting the rear of the trailer, fifty-five feet behind him, hit the low spot in the swale and started to dig in. The drag on the wheels jerked the tractor and trailer back into a straight line.

By now the engine was screaming so loudly that CC thought it might throw a rod. The drive wheels were spinning, but the truck was only creeping forward. Afraid to try to shift gears because he might stall the engine or blow out the transmission, he simply kept his foot on the accelerator. The back wheels of the trailer hit the uphill bank of the swale with a bounce, cleared the worse spot, started to slip sideways again, leveled off, and cleared the ditch.

Even in the midst of the truck's almost uncontrollable career, CC was thinking of the fuel being gulped down by that roaring engine. He began to let up on the pedal as the cab roared between the last two tall hemlocks that stood in the shadow of the cliff. The truck was now slightly askew the desired path, but CC kept the drive wheels turning as fast as he could without causing them to spin. The steering wheel was jerking back and forth in his hands, and with pine boughs slapping against the windshield, he could barely see where he was going. Risking the possibility that the pilot of that plane would see the rig beneath the trees, he reached out with his left hand and turned on the headlights.

A glance back in his west coast mirror showed the side of the trailer about to drag against a tree on his left, and he floored the pedal. The rig again straightened out, but the trailer scraped against a broken limb, making a deep crease along its upper side. Why, he wondered, did that make me think of the iceberg that tore the life from the hull of the Titanic? That random thought fled as the rig pulled free, passing deeper into the shadows of the narrow defile, and rolling ahead over the saplings and small cedars like some Brobdingnagian giant as he steered it toward the watergate. In spite of the crawling pace of the wheels, the jarring movement of the vehicle through the twilit underbrush made the movements seem both precipitous and frightening.

The idyllic little lake flashed into view, captured in the sweep of the headlight's beams. Beyond it he saw the stream that fed the lake, the water dancing in the sunset, careening over rocks and ledges before coming to temporary rest in the lake. Even though he was several hundred yards away, he could see that it was dizzying in its motion. He steered to the right, moving around the place where the water gathered before it poured into the culvert pipe.

The left front wheel of his tractor was now perilously close to the retaining wall into which the culvert pipe was fixed, and, at one point the eroding bank began to crumble under the heavy trailer's wheels. He drew the rig to a stop, turned off the lights, set the brake, shut down the engine, and sat there shaking with excitement and fatigue. Yet, he realized, he had no time to rest.

Also from Frank Becker

For my friends concerned about the future of the Church and your place in it, and for those of you who are concerned with emergency preparedness, these are both available in paper and as e-books.

Paige Patterson — past president of the Southern Baptist Convention, and president of America's largest seminary — wrote: “In a day of 'how-to' manuals on church growth and effectiveness, to find a writer who tells the truth...is a breath of fresh air.... Frank Becker...has clearly enunciated the one essential, namely, a return to the church of the New Testament.”

And Dr. John Kenzy. who co-founded the Teen Challenge Bible Institute with the late David Wilkerson, called The Depression Proof Church “Compelling and timely,” and said that it “exposes revelation from God.”

Senator Stephen R. Wise, PhD, called it “hard hitting,”

"inspiring a return to biblical practices that have been forsaken in a lust for ever larger churches."

And the Jacksonville Theological Seminary created a course called, The Depression Proof Church, for students at every level.

You Can Triumph Over Terror

Special Agent Frank Gil (Retired) FECR PD; featured on COPS, Metro-Dade Special Response Team (SWAT) wrote: "Frank's book should be required reading. By preparing, you increase your chances of survival, facilitate our ability to assist you, and reduce your own stress and anxiety."

John, Sipos, Broadcast Journalist and host of "Hour Tampa Bay," wrote, "If you apply the ideas in this book...you and your family will radically improve your prospects for survival."

The Chronicles of CC:

War's Desolation (Thanksgiving, 2013)
The Heav'n Rescued Land (December, 2013)
Freemen Shall Stand (Scheduled, early, 2014)
Our Cause It Is Just (Scheduled, mid-2014)

Made in the USA
Charleston, SC
23 January 2014